GUNSMOKE LEGEND

GUNSMOKE LEGEND

Ja　’age was a living legend – a Union Army
sh　shooter, scout, Indian fighter and US
m　s’ al. Ash Colter, by contrast, was a mild-
m　ered orphan. They were complete
o]　ites, and yet theirs was a partnership
f　in blood. These were the men who
　ed the famous Snake River Shootout;
n who led Colonel George Armstrong
to one of his most controversial
es against the Cheyenne; the men who
the hell-towns of Kansas and Dakota
ry. They were as close as brothers and
ey were on opposite sides of the fence
the time came for the final, bloody
lown.

GUNSMOKE
LEGEND

by

Matt Logan

Dales Large Print Books
Long Preston, North Yorkshire,
BD23 4ND, England.

British Library Cataloguing in Publication Data.

Logan, Matt
    Gunsmoke legend.

    A catalogue record of this book is
    available from the British Library

    ISBN   978-1-84262-783-9 pbk

First published in Great Britain in 1993 by Robert Hale Limited

Copyright © Matt Logan 1993

Cover illustration © Richard Clifton-Day by arrangement with Alison Eldred

Published in Large Print 2010 by arrangement with
David Whitehead

Dales Large Print is an imprint of Library Magna Books Ltd.

Printed and bound in Great Britain by
T.J. (International) Ltd., Cornwall, PL28 8RW

Dedicated to the memory of my Dad,
who was a gunsmoke legend
in his own right.

ONE

'Forgive me for asking, sir,' said the young, plain-faced waitress, as she ran her cloth swiftly across the small, scratched table at which he was sitting. 'But would your name by any chance be … Page?'

He regarded her curiously out of his glittering blue eyes, for he imagined himself to be unknown in these parts. She was only eighteen or nineteen, perhaps not even as old as that, and she had fine auburn hair set in ringlets and skin that was as pale as milk. He did not think she posed any threat to him, so he said, 'It would indeed,' in his quiet, formal, well-enunciated way, adding a question of his own. 'Might I ask as to why you enquire?'

She straightened up and looked down at him. She appeared very worried. After a brief, jerky nod and a glance out through the window into Le Quince's single street, she said, 'Two men were in here earlier this morning. While I … was out back, preparing their breakfast, they began to talk. They didn't know that I could hear what they were saying.'

Page's lean face showed only polite interest. 'And?' he prompted.

'They … they were plotting to kill a man they knew to be coming this way,' she went on, trying to pour all her words out in a rush. 'A man named Jack Page. You, sir.'

He smiled to ease some of her agitation, and the movement of his lips twisted up his long, flowing moustache. 'Did they, indeed?' he mused, apparently unconcerned by the revelation. 'And did they say *why* they were going to do this thing?'

Another nod. 'They said you were a sharpshooter, sir. For the Union Army. They said you had picked off as many as fifty of their men with as many bullets, sir, and all in the one day. They said that you were too good at your job to be allowed to live.'

He shrugged modestly, considering what the girl had said. It was true, he allowed. He *was* good at his job, quite possibly the best damn' marksman in the whole of the Union Army. The story of his picking off fifty men was something of an exaggeration, certainly. But had he not voluntarily participated in that altercation the Rebs called Elkhorn Tavern and his own side referred to as the Battle of Pea Ridge? Had he not ridden four horses into the ground, running messages back and forth behind enemy lines? Had he not found himself a spot on Cross Timber Hollow and killed thirty-five of the enemy from hiding?

At last his eyes grew sharp again and he fixed the girl with a close scrutiny. 'And did you by any chance also happen to overhear how they planned to kill me?' he asked.

She wrung her cloth desperately in her little hands. 'Yes sir. They are going to wait until you have your food before you, and then one of them is going to come in through the front door and the other is going to come in through the rear. They plan to catch you in a cross-fire and murder you.'

Page looked around their rather drab surroundings. 'That would explain why I am at present your only customer,' he muttered. 'Even though this *is* the supper hour.' His smile vanished quite without warning, and ice began to coagulate in his eyes. 'Very good, little girl. You have done well, and will not find me ungenerous in the matter of reward.'

Her relief was obvious. 'You will leave, then? While you still can?'

'And disappoint my would-be executioners? I fear not, little girl.' Beneath the moustache, Page's smile came back. 'No, I will trouble you for a steak, some corn fritters and a generous portion of black-eyed peas instead. Pecan pie to follow, and plenty of good, hot coffee.'

She looked down at him incredulously. Was he mad? Did he not know the meaning of fear?

'Run along, girl,' he said gently.

The young waitress did as she was told, weaving back through the maze of tables to the counter, and the kitchen beyond, sorry now that she had involved herself in this business. If what those other men had said was true, then this man, this Page, was himself a killer, and should pay for his crimes. But hearing those whispered plottings had made her feel sick this morning. Murder ... it was an awful word, and an even worse deed! She could not allow herself to become a party to it. A terrible, killing madness had already overtaken her country since the outbreak of war. She did not want to be a part of further killing. And so, perhaps by warning this tall, big-chested man with long, golden-brown hair and the tilted sombrero, she had hoped to save a life instead of see it taken.

But this Jack Page had made no move to rise and leave the restaurant, as she had expected. Instead he had asked for a meal!

She busied herself at the range, glancing up every so often to regard him through the doorless aperture. He had called her a little girl, she remembered, and yet he was only young himself, not even twenty-five yet. He had entered the restaurant in a string of graceful, flowing movements, and if his long black frock coat, silk waistcoat and crimson sash were anything to go by, he was something of a fashion-plate.

Covertly she studied his face. It was long, thin, pale, with pronounced cheekbones and a well-defined jaw. He was, she thought with a blush, quite handsome. His moustache covered the narrow line of his mouth and stretched in a downturned horseshoe to his chin. He seemed quite content sitting there in the centre of his restaurant. In fact, he had closed his very blue eyes and appeared to be dozing.

She frowned when she saw that, for surely he could not have misunderstood her warning, or the gravity of the situation?

She fixed his meal and took the laden plate outside. When she set it down before him, her hands were trembling. 'I'm obliged,' he said politely as he picked up his knife and fork. 'Now, get you to one side. I would not wish for you to get hurt in the overflow.'

Dutifully she went around behind the counter and began to polish it with her cloth, not really concentrating on the task.

The seconds ticked away. Still he just sat at the table in the centre of the restaurant, slicing up his steak. *Why don't you get up and go?* she asked him silently. *Go on – now, while you still have the chance!* She looked through the front window to the big black gelding tied to the rack outside. The horse looked as sleek and powerful as its owner. It would carry him far from this town and the danger in it, if only he would see sense and leave.

But still he sat there, cutting and forking up food, as if he had not a care in the world.

Her eyes darted nervously to the yellow-faced wall-clock. It was a little past six. Barely twelve hours had elapsed since those two men had come in this morning, and yet it seemed as if the day had lasted a lifetime.

She thought she heard a noise – a creaking floorboard. The sound made her start. But then silence settled back over the restaurant. She must have been mistaken.

The wall-clock went *tick, tock, tick, tock...*

The girl did not think she could take much more of this waiting game. Her nerves were beginning to get the better of her. Why, she thought she might actually swoon.

Tick, tock, tick, tock...

Entirely without warning, a tall skinny man burst in through the front door with a long-barrelled gun blazing in his left hand, and at the same moment his partner came in through the kitchen doorway, screaming foul abuse and triggering his own weapon.

The girl screamed and dropped behind the relative safety of the counter and Jack Page powered up out of his chair and spun to face the first of his attackers with his hands already folding around the grips of the Remington New Model Army .44s tucked butt-forward in his sash.

The girl heard his chairlegs shuddering against the floorboards, the chair itself finally tumble over. He stepped calmly to one side, thumbed back the hammer on one gun, then the other, and began to return fire.

The glass window shattered with a sharp crash. A bullet thudded into the counter, making the young girl scream all the louder.

Still Page and his attackers continued to trade shots.

Gunsmoke began to drift up to the tin ceiling and fog the air. The would-be assassins kept screaming abuse.

Then–

Two .44-calibre balls slammed into the first man's chest and all his ear-splitting invective turned suddenly to a screech of pain. As blood ribboned out of him in a crimson damburst he went backwards like a rag doll, right through the front door with a crash of splintering glass, and sprawled dead on the boardwalk outside.

At last Page turned to face his second attacker, going down into a crouch now but still just as calm as the calmest summer's day. He brought his right-hand Remington up, thumbed back the hammer, fired it, repeated the procedure with the one in his left, then triggered the right again.

The guns thundered–

boom! boom! boom! boom!

–one after the other.

Page jerked as he took a bullet-crease in the left bicep, but gave no other sign that he'd been hit.

The exchange of gunfire went on and on and on.

At last the second man twitched under the impact of two bullets, hunched up, clutched himself, dropped his gun, fell to the floor and then squirmed around for a while like some enormous snake. His breath sawed in and out quickly. To the young girl he sounded like a dog panting. Then he stopped breathing altogether and absolute silence pressed in on the young girl's ears.

She remained exactly where she was, hunkered down beneath the counter, shivering. She felt a damp warmth at her crotch and knew with shame that she had wet herself in her terror. After a long, indeterminate time she heard footsteps sounding heavy and ponderous, coming closer. Left foot, right foot, left foot, right foot... They stopped just the other side of the counter.

'I am beholden to you, little girl,' Jack Page said from someplace up above her. She stayed right where she was, unable to move even if she'd wanted to, huddled up, hands clasped over her head, arms pressed tight to her ears to try and drown out the thunder of gunfire. 'I regret very much that this unpleasantness had to occur in your fine eatery.'

She still remained hidden from view.

'You will, I trust, find enough money in the pockets of these bushwhackers to pay for the repair of your establishment. This here is for you. My way of saying thank you.'

She heard him set some coins down on the counter.

He turned away then, and walked slowly back around all the empty tables, left foot, right foot, left foot, right foot, and a moment afterwards she heard the shattered door open, then close, followed by the beat of his horse's hoofs as he rode steadily away into the approaching night.

TWO

I would not say that Jack Page was a liar, exactly. No man in his right mind would ever dare. But he was what I would call a vain man, and when the lie painted a more flattering portrait of him than the truth ... well, Jack had no qualms about adopting the lie. Neither did it help when, towards the end of his life, the yellow-jacket novelists from back East discovered him and embroidered upon an already well-fabricated tale.

Thus it has, over the years, become almost impossible to sort the wheat from the chaff in the matter of Jack Page. But there are some parts of his history that we do know for a fact. That he was born on the first day of March, 1837, and raised in Walker's

Crossing, Illinois, for example. That his father, William, was a moderately successful farmer, and that Jack himself was the youngest of fourteen children.

The gullible American public has long been led to believe that Jack was born with the spirit of adventure running through his veins. But, like so much of the myth that obscures the real man, this was not so. In fact, Jack was a sickly child who was visited by all manner of illnesses in his formative years. That he came close to death on several occasions and yet still somehow managed to survive and grow all the stronger for it does go to show, however, that even at that age he possessed some of the stubborn, whipcord-toughness which came to mark his succeeding decades.

Similarly, it is true that Jack left home at an early age. But this was not, as writers such as Mr Buntline and Colonel Travers would have us believe, because he got into a fight over a girl and nearly killed his opponent, although I will grant you that this story is infinitely more colourful than the truth. The fact is that Jack's father was a rather pious individual, and Jack, who was anything *but* pious, often found life in his father's house oppressive.

Thus it was that he came to set out upon his travels at the tender age of sixteen or so, although it has to be said that he did not remain tender for very long. By the time he wound up in Kansas and became part of General Jim Lane's Free State Militia, he had already gained something of a reputation as a first-class fighting man. And not just with his fists, either, although he was handy enough with those. No, sir. You could give Jack practically any weapon and he would master it in next to no time. He had what you would call an aptitude for such things. He could be the gentlest man on the face of the earth, and yet God had seen fit to bless him – if that is the right word – with a talent for killing – a talent, in fact, that was soon discovered by those dirty-fighting, slave-holding Missouri Border Ruffians, many to their cost.

Jack was also something of a ladies' man, and I swear to hear him tell it that he fell in and out of love more than a dozen times before he was twenty. One story says that he fell in love with a half-Shawnee girl in the late '50s, and lived for a time as that most reviled of species, the squaw man, but since I do not know the exact truth of that, I will not comment upon it further. I will say, however, that Jack Page was about the handsomest man I ever saw, and he knew it, too. He attracted women without even trying, and enjoyed their subsequent attentions to the full. Like I said, he was a vain man.

When the War broke out, he volunteered to serve as a scout for the Army of the Southwest, though he seldom spoke much of those days in southwestern Missouri, Kansas and Oklahoma – Indian Territory as it was known back then. I do know for a fact that his proficiency with firearms soon elevated him to the position of sharpshooter, however, and that once his skill at picking off the enemy became common knowledge, the long-suffering Confederate forces made several attempts to assassinate him.

In due course he found favour with his superiors and eventually undertook several hazardous missions for the Union Army – guiding supply trains safely through enemy lines, finding out troop strengths and movements and the like. All through the years he served with the Union Army as scout, spy and sharpshooter, however, he did so strictly as a volunteer, and never as an enlisted man.

After the War, he went to work for the Overland Stage Company, tooling coaches along the Santa Fe Trail, but within a year he was leading freight-trains up from New Mexico to Independence, Missouri, for those enterprising purveyors Russell, Majors and Waddell. It was whilst he was thus employed that another of his more famous exploits took place, and it was indirectly because of it that our trails eventually crossed and I came to call him my close friend.

Jack had just started to lead his wagons through Raton Pass, New Mexico, when he wisely decided to ride on ahead to check the lie of the land. For those among you who have never travelled that stretch of the country, I can tell you that it is a hard, twisting, tricky trail, with steep rock walls and sparse vegetation, and there are some parts of it that are so dangerous that only one wagon at a time should ever attempt to cross them.

Anyway, there was Jack, riding on ahead, when suddenly there appeared out of some stunted pines fifty or sixty feet ahead of him, an enormous grizzly bear.

Seeing the beast, Jack's horse at once reared up in surprise and threw him. He landed hard by the edge of the trail, lost himself momentarily in a cloud of dust and then quickly regained his feet.

Now, as any man with any sense will tell you, you do not tangle with bears if there is any chance at all that you can avoid it. And whilst it is true that they are critters of usually placid disposition, even one of their more playful taps is likely to knock you into the middle of next week. More often than not, it is enough just to let the bear know you have seen him and acknowledge his right to be there. Pretty soon after that, once he is convinced that you mean him no harm, he will lose interest in you and go on his way.

But this old silvertip was different.

It is possible that he was just born ornery, or maybe he was getting old and crotchety. They go like that sometimes, if their teeth are wearing out and paining them, or if they have a wound that's festering.

There are any number of possible reasons why that bear just stood there in the middle of the trail. Maybe it was just too plain lazy to get up and move out of the way. Maybe he was spoiling for a fight. Maybe *he* was really a *she,* intent on protecting her cubs.

Whichever, the thing just stood there on all fours, watching Jack through its piggy little black eyes. And, after a time, it loosed off a bellow and stood up on its hind legs.

Well, to hear Jack tell it afterwards, that bear was so tall he like to've bumped his head against the sky when he did that. And certainly I myself have seen bears not even fully-grown top eight or even ten feet.

By this time, Jack's horse had run back down the trail, leaving him to face the grizzly a-foot. And from the way the grizzly was screwing up its snout to reveal its long, yellow teeth, it didn't seem likely that he was fixing to ask Jack to dance. All things considered, it was not really the best position in which a fellow could hope to find himself, but Jack, ever the fighter, decided to make at least some token display of resistance.

He planted himself there in the white, settling dust and yelled at the bear to get the hell out of there. He took off his sombrero and waved it around a bit, just for good measure. But the bear remained singularly unimpressed by this show of bravado. In fact, he came a couple of paces nearer.

Jack swallowed. He couldn't just stand around here all day until the bear decided to move on, and likewise he knew that if he turned tail and ran, the bear would outrun him with ease. If that happened, then the consequences hardly bore consideration.

The bear came another few paces closer.

It was then that Jack made a fateful decision. He walked out to meet the beast, just as bold as brass, and waved his sombrero about some more. I guess he was hoping to call that silvertip's bluff. You know, to say, 'All right. Come ahead, if you like. You don't scare me.'

Trouble was, the bear called *his* bluff instead.

It came down onto all fours and started to come at him in a lumbering run.

Jack froze. The sound of its growl and the sight of its snout folding up in a defiant snarl transfixed him, and he watched, open-mouthed, as better than a thousand pounds of sharp-clawed, massively strong killing machine came thundering straight at him.

At last he thought to grab his .44s and start blasting away at the oncoming giant. He saw little puffs of dust fly up off its barbed brown coat every time a bullet struck home. Around them, the pass fairly vibrated to the sound of gunblast after gunblast. Soon the bear's fur was stippled with blood.

But still the creature came on.

And Jack Page's guns ran dry.

With a roar, the bear lunged up and knocked him to one side with a sweep of its left paw. Jack went crashing into the rocks fringing the trail, lost his hat and guns and very nearly his consciousness too. He tried to scramble back to his feet, but even as he did so, the bear's shadow fell across him and the bear itself swatted him some more.

Jack staggered giddily, knowing that if he *did* pass out, he was finished. His only chance was to try and keep out of reach, perhaps retrieve and reload his guns and put a few more bullets into his opponent to stop his clock once and for all.

Before he could do any such thing, however, the bear fairly hurled itself at him and he went down beneath it in another explosion of dust. Afterwards, he told me that the impact fair knocked the wind from his sails, as you might expect, and that he saw more stars than the universe could ever possibly possess.

Now, it is true that the bear was, by this time, severely wounded, but it seems that he was determined to take his killer down to Hades with him. It's hardly surprising, then, that Jack had one or two things to say about that.

For a moment they were caught up in a life-or-death struggle there on the rocky ground. Jack, buried beneath the blood-splattered, writhing bear, was trapped in a world where there was no light and even less air, a world that stank of bear-sweat and death, where the only sounds were his own laboured breathing and the constant snarl and growl of his enemy.

In desperation, he managed to reach one hand down to his sash and claw out his Bowie knife, a formidable weapon with a very heavy blade.

With a yell of rage, he thrust the knife up into the bear's belly, and the bear loosed a bellow of pain.

Again and again Jack plunged his blade hilt-deep into the bear's thick, blocky torso, until its steaming blood flowed like hot rain down upon his body.

The bear fell away from him with a rumble of fury, considerably weakened by the onslaught and now only minutes from death, but still it managed to lash out at him, its wicked, four-inch claws ploughing deep, serious furrows in his arms, legs, scalp and body.

But if that old bear was a tenacious sonofabitch, it was in for a surprise, for they didn't come any more tenacious than Jack Page. Badly injured though he was, he was damned if he was going to give up now.

Briefly the bear came up onto its hind legs again, and Jack saw with revulsion that he had almost disembowelled the beast. The bear sank back onto all fours almost at once, and then keeled over onto its side.

Half-crazed by the combat and loss of blood, Jack went over and threw himself upon it, stabbing and hacking for all he was worth. The bear's howls mixed with Jack's screams as he plunged the blade in again and again and again, cutting the creature's throat and mincing up its exposed innards, until at length reason returned and he realised that the bear was about as dead as it was likely to get.

He collapsed upon the corpse then and the Bowie blade slipped from his trembling hand. When the first of the wagon drivers found him about half an hour later, he was in such bad shape that there was considerable doubt among them that he would pull through.

Still, they did what they could for him. They washed him down and bandaged him up and put him in the back of one of the freight-heavy wagons and took him back south, thinking that they would be more likely to enlist the services of a mortician than a medic at the first town they came to.

But that wasn't the first time Jack Page proved other men wrong, and medical science being what it is, he was eventually put back together and sent by the company to recuperate up at the Snake River Station in northwest Nebraska – and that is where I first came to meet him.

THREE

I am not apt to forget the day I began my long association with Jack Page. It was the first day of March 1867 – the day Nebraska became the thirty-seventh state of the Union.

We had already heard about Jack's run-in with the bear, of course. That kind of story has a way of travelling. We had also heard that, after the doctors in Santa Fe had done as much for him as they could, it had been left to cleverer heads in Kansas City to put him more firmly upon the road to recovery.

It was then that the powers-that-be at Russell, Majors and Waddell decided to send him out to us for recuperation, though I am still not quite certain as to why; we were a very busy station in those days, and in addition to providing a change of horses for the coaches plying the east-west trail, and food and shelter for the passengers, we also operated a combination store and saloon for the cattlemen who lived in the vicinity. However, Horace Traylor, who managed the station, had been told to give him light duties when he arrived, tending to the stock and such, until his constitution showed some sign of returning to its former vigour.

It occurs to me that perhaps I should introduce myself before I take my narrative any further, though I will confess at the outset that there is not really all that much to tell. My name is Ashley Colter, called Ash. I was born on a small farm in Iowa in 1848. My father was a tall, broad, powerful man who, like me, was sometimes awkward in company. I still remember his large, ruddy face and his easy laugh, though the memory still grows more vague with every passing year. My mother, by contrast, was a small woman;

pale, pretty, humourless and over-protective, with one strand of faded blonde hair forever hanging down across her forehead.

My childhood was happy and uncomplicated, although things grew progressively more difficult once papa went away to war in '61. He had been such a big, tireless man that he had done the work of two. Now it was all down to one sickly woman and a thirteen year-old boy. Long days, I remember. Long, hard days filled with ploughing, sowing, planting, reaping, taking our meagre crops to market.

Then, one fine afternoon in the late summer of 1863, a one-legged soldier riding a ribby, tucked-up horse brought the news that papa had been killed at Vicksburg back in July.

Even now I can see the worn-out, tired look on the man's malnourished, bewhiskered face, the tears misting in his eyes as he talked for a while to mama, the thump-shuffle-thump way he got around on his one crutch when mama finally remembered her manners and asked him to light. He'd stayed the night at our small cabin and left early the following morning, after mama gave him a food parcel and helped him mount the horse.

Mama started looking at me differently from then on. Maybe some dark cloud in my sky-blue eyes betrayed me and she read my unspoken desire to go out into the world and kill the rebel scum who'd murdered my father a thousand miles from home. Maybe she was afraid that I would run away to do exactly that; that she would end up losing *me*, as well.

I think that was why we left the farm not so long afterwards, and simply travelled with no real destination or purpose in mind; so that she could occupy me with other, less vengeful thoughts. Or maybe the prospect of continuing to live on the farm without papa was just too much for her to bear.

Whichever it was, that was exactly what we did; quit the farm and travelled, stopping briefly whenever we needed to find work and rebuild our dwindling resources. Sweeping, digging, washing, picking; anything would do, and *did,* until at last the war drew to a finish and some kind of order settled back over our ravaged country.

By then, however, mama had contracted some kind of lung fever, and she died within a month of war's end.

I was seventeen then, tall for my age but as ribby and tucked-up as that one-legged soldier's poor horse. I was indrawn and rootless, too; set even further adrift now, with the loss of my mother.

I drifted for a time across this vast, untamed country, before ending up as a kind of stablehand-cum-labourer there at the Snake River Station. I enjoyed my life there. It was the closest thing I'd had to a permanent home for nearly four years, and the other employees – Mr Traylor and his common-law wife Hetty, and Cy Pollack, who ran the saloon and store – the closest thing to family.

It was, as I have said, a busy crossing, and there were always chores to do. The station itself was a sturdy log structure built in a long, low L-shape, with the passengers' common room occupying one branch and the store occupying the other. Our own quarters were located at the rear of the building, and just across the other side of the dirt yard stood the stable and corrals.

And it was a very pleasant spot in which to live and work, for we had the Snake River to our backs and good open grassland to front and sides, with stands of timber to act as windbreaks. The summer was my favourite time, for there was always work to be done outdoors. In winter, the elements forced us to stay inside and huddle around the stove, and though they were decent enough men, I did not always care to spend day after unrelieved day in the company of Mr Traylor and Cy Pollack.

Jack Page came to us on the noon stage from Franklin that crisp first day of March, and like excited schoolchildren we lined up, the four of us, to watch his arrival. The coach was about two hours late as I recall, but when it finally came into view around the shoulder of a low hill about a quarter of a mile out, red body rocking and swaying, yellow wheels appearing to spin in reverse, I think we all felt the same expectant thrill wash through us.

Jim Ballew and Curly Thomas were up in the box, Jim cracking his whip high above the heads of his straining six-horse team. It was a sight that never failed to inspire me, and that day was no different. The coach came bouncing toward us, following the gentle curve of the trail with dust billowing up behind it and the horses, with their flapping and flowing manes, leaning hard into harness.

Then Jim was applying the brake and the entire rig was slewing to an unsteady halt before us.

'Afternoon, folks!' Jim Ballew called down, slipping his whip into its socket and throwing me his reins so that I might begin changing the team.

'Good trip?' asked Horace Traylor.

'Tol'able.'

He and Curly Thomas hopped down from the box and stretched their spines, then headed straight for the dining room, where Hetty had a big pot of rabbit stew heating up.

I stood there beside the heaving, lathery team waiting for the passengers to climb out into the good bright afternoon sunshine. After a moment the nearside door swung open and a middle-aged woman climbed down. A man of similar age followed her, then a younger man in a sharp grey suit. But I knew instinctively that this was not the man we had heard so much about. I knew that when he finally put in an appearance, there would be something about him that set him apart from other men, something special. And neither was I wrong.

The passengers shook the cricks out of their backs and the middle-aged woman muttered some comment about how Jim Ballew ought to moderate his speed when travelling over such uneven roads, but I don't believe any of us paid her much mind.

We were all too busy just hovering around there, each of us waiting for the same thing.

At last the coach creaked a little on its leather straps and the last of the passengers stepped down into the yard, and he was everything we had imagined he would be, and quite possibly a bit more besides.

The first thing I guess anyone noticed about Jack Page was his hair. Golden brown it was, wavy and worn unfashionably long. Then you saw his thick, flowing moustache. After that you noticed the sheer size of the man, for he was a good six feet two.

After that several things came to the eye in a rush; his lean, pale face, with its prominent cheekbones and pointed jaw, the glittering blue of his eyes, the broad chest, narrow hips, long legs.

He moved like a cat, I thought as I watched him close the coach door behind him and turn to look at us with the faintest glimmer of amusement stirring in his eyes. And he had that same predatory *something* that you so often find in cats, too; as if he were a born hunter, forever stealing an unsuspecting prey.

What surprised me most about him, I think, was his mode of dress, for I had expected him to be some kind of rugged frontiersman. What I saw instead resembled nothing so much as a dude. He wore a black frock coat over a boiled white shirt, a string tie and silk vest. His trousers were of a rather loud check, and worn over flat-heeled towns-man's shoes. When he moved, however, I could just see the walnut grips of his matched Remingtons peeking butt-forward from out of the crimson sash encircling his waist, and I thought, *He is a cross-draw man, then.*

'Mr Page?' Horace Traylor said after a moment.

Jack inclined his head. Even then he had something haughty and regal about him. Horace stepped forward and shook with him, then made the introductions. When he came to Hetty, Jack swept off his hat, took one of her hands in his, bowed low and kissed it softly. Hetty was so taken aback by this display of chivalry that she very nearly swooned, but somehow she managed to recover and curtsied instead. When he shook hands with me, I found his grip to be firm, cool and dependable, and when he said, 'I'm pleased to make your acquaintance, young man,' I felt enormously privileged, as if he had bestowed a great honour upon me just by acknowledging my right to be there.

Once the formalities had been observed, Mr Traylor told him to get his carpetbag and saddle out of the boot of the coach. Then he showed him to his quarters, and after that something like normality returned to the Snake River Station.

The next time I saw him, Jack was dressed in a hickory shirt and buckskin pants and a good strong pair of working boots, and that seemed altogether more fitting attire for the duties he had come here to undertake. He was a gregarious fellow, as we soon found out, and once he got to know us better, which did not take long, he was quite happy to satisfy our curiosity on all kinds of matters. In fact, he was never happier than when he had an audience, and although he did more than his fair share around the station, it seemed that he was never too busy to regale us with tales both tall and true.

I took a shine to him at once. Having lost my father so early in life, I tended to enjoy the company of older men because they reminded me of him, and in Jack Page I found a companion who suited this particular need right down to the ground. I hesitate to say that our relationship became akin to that of a father and his son. More closely I would approximate it to that of two brothers who also happen to be very good friends.

A couple of days after he arrived, I exercised some of the horses in the corral. If you keep horses stabled up for any length of time, they can sometimes get a little nervous about going out into the open again, and you have the devil's own job trying to coax them. So I always tried to make it a point to exercise them out of doors as often as I could.

On this particular day I had been fussing

around with some of them when I suddenly realised that I was being watched. Turning around, I found Jack sitting astride the corral fence, fingering his moustache. Nudging my hat to the back of my head and running a forearm down across my sweating face, I went over to him, for as I have already said, I was always happy to be in his company.

'You have an affinity with horseflesh,' he noted when I was near enough.

I shrugged. 'I try. But sometimes they take a lot of understanding.'

'I'm having my own horse brought out in a week or so,' he said. 'You'll like him, Ash. He's as black as night, and yet his temperament is as bright as day. He's a pure Tennessee thoroughbred.'

A fellow from Franklin fetched the horse out a week later, and it was everything Jack Page had said it would be, a magnificent beast that stood no less than seventeen hands at the shoulder. I rode it once, with Jack's permission, but the horse had been trained well and it was basically a one-man animal.

When I think back to those first few weeks in Jack's company, I remember only a charming, affable, gentle man. Jack Page might not be very good at listening to others, but he was always the first in line to lend a hand or offer advice.

Then, one day, Walt Devlin, Devlin's brother Hal and their sister's husband Tom Farson rode in for supplies, and I saw a darker side to his nature.

Walt Devlin was a big brawler of a man, forty-one years of age and sour of temperament. He ran cattle over a sizeable stretch of the country, and had spent many of his earlier years fighting tooth and nail to hold his land from those men, red and white, who would take it from him. He did this with the help of a pretty rough crew, including his brother and brother-in-law, who themselves were no beginners when it came to a rough-house or gunplay. Devlin it was, in fact, who had sold this very stretch of land to the stage-coach company a couple of years earlier.

I am not sure that Devlin came in looking

for trouble that day, but if I had to make an educated guess, I would allow that there was a distinct possibility.

He and the others came in late one afternoon in early April. It was their first visit to the place since Jack had arrived six weeks earlier. As they reined down in the yard, they could not fail to see him, for he was busy with a hammer and nails, performing some minor repairs to the stable walls. I was watching them from one of the common room's small windows, and I saw from their expressions that he had aroused their curiosity. Ever suspicious of newcomers, the Devlins were wondering just who he was.

Then Horace Traylor came out of the common room to greet them. 'Afternoon, Walt. Boys. How's things?'

Devlin and his kin dismounted. They were big men, the Devlins, and thick-set. Walt himself had a squarish face, hazel eyes, a once-broken nose and a broad, thick-lipped mouth. Hal, who was a couple of years his junior, favoured him considerably, although his features were somewhat narrower and a little more appealing. They had hair as black as midnight, those two; Walt's was just turning snowy at the temples. As for Tom Farson; well, he was a little cock-bantam of a fellow, slim and wiry, with a freckled, pinched-in face and sandy hair.

Walt jerked a thumb in Jack's direction and said, 'New feller?'

After a glance over his shoulder, Mr Traylor nodded. 'That's Jack,' he explained. 'Been with us about a month or so now. Stock tender.' He paused, then said, 'You boys come in for supplies or whiskey?'

It was obvious that they'd come in for supplies, for Tom Farson was trailing a packmule behind him, but I think Mr Traylor just wanted to steer the subject away from Jack, because he knew those boys had a reputation for hoorawing newcomers.

'Both,' Walt said gruffly.

Mr Traylor put a hand on his arm and said, with forced bonhomie, 'Well, let's get to it, then.'

But Walt stayed put and raised his voice instead. 'Hey, stock tender,' he called. He had a voice like gravel, that one. It was a harsh, almost painful thing to hear. I often wondered how his woman, Kate Spickett, who had a place about a dozen miles further down the trail, ever put up with him. 'Come take these here horses.'

Jack stopped what he'd been doing and turned to regard Walt over one shoulder. A moment later he set down his hammer and nails and came across, graceful as ever, to take their proffered reins. Walt glared at him, for no other reason than that he always tried to intimidate everyone he met. It was just the way he was. Jack only smiled lazily back at him, and the insolence in the gesture was plain.

Mr Traylor, sensing the mood, tried to keep things sociable. 'Jack, this here is Walt Devlin,' he said. 'Walt runs the Lazy D, biggest spread in these parts. Walt, this is Jack–'

'Just take good care o' my horse, stock tender,' Walt cut in, looking his man right in the eye.

Jack shrugged mildly then dipped his head. 'I try to take good care of *all* the horses ... *Mr* Devlin.' And without waiting for a reply, he led the animals off towards the stable.

'Surly cuss, ain't he?' muttered Walt.

Mr Traylor spread his hands and said uncomfortably, 'Well, you know...'

'He got the look of a troublemaker to me,' opined Hal. 'You see all them scratches an' cuts on his face an' hands? He's been in a fight, an' not so long ago, neither.'

'He a-one for fightin', Horace?' Walt asked, interested because he was a bit of a pugilist himself. 'Don't tell me you're hirin' troublemakers around here now?'

Mr Traylor's laugh was a little strangled. 'You know me better'n that, Walt. The company wouldn't stand for it. Come on, now, let's get inside. I'll spring for the first round.'

They stamped across the yard and entered the store. It was a long, dark structure, filled with sacks and barrels and crates, and a couple of tables where cattlemen or men just passing through could sit and play cards or eat. Cy Pollack sold just about everything in there, including passable whiskey and, when he could get it, real St Louis beer. He was waiting for them at the counter down at the far end of the place, hands spread flat against the scratched, ring-marked wood. 'What'll it be, fellers?' he asked.

'Whiskey all round,' said Mr Traylor. As they bellied up to the bar, he added conversationally, 'You'd be busy right now, I expect, what with calf-cropping and all.'

'Ayuh,' agreed Hal. 'They's never enough hours in the day.'

'Well, I don't know about you, Hal,' said Tom. 'But my workin' day's long enough just as it is, thank you kindly.'

Mr Traylor relaxed a little, for the boys seemed to be in a good mood for a change. 'But you're never too busy to come on in and wet your whistles, is that it?' he asked with a wink.

They were on their second round when Jack entered the store and strode up to them. He had a very deliberate walk, did Jack. It was a slow, easy, confident thing, and every time I saw him walk any distance, I felt that there was nothing yet created that could stop him from getting where he wanted to go, nor even make him break stride.

Walt and the others turned inquisitively and watched him come ahead. As he came to a halt before Walt he dipped his head politely and said, 'Excuse me, Mr Devlin.'

A grin spread lazily across Walt's lumpy face. He said, 'All right, stock tender – you're excused.'

His kin thought that was a real caution, and their laughter came out loud and braying.

Jack merely stood his ground and waited for the merriment to die down. 'It's about your horse,' he said at length. 'I noticed she was favouring her right foreleg. She's wearing an ill-fitting shoe and I'd say she strained the muscle trying to go easy on it.'

Walt sobered and narrowed his eyes. 'Is

that a fact?' he asked in a low voice.

'It's a fact,' Jack replied evenly. 'If I were you, I'd go easy on her on the way home, else you could make the damage worse. She might go lame altogether.'

'I fitted them shoes myself, stock tender,' Walt said.

Jack inclined his shoulders. 'Well, maybe you should have left it to a professional.'

'Are you sayin', I don't know how to shoe a horse?'

'I'm saying you'd do well to have that shoe pulled and replaced, that's all. And to spare your horse from any long, hard riding until she recovers.'

He was just about to turn away and leave them to it when Walt looked at Mr Traylor and said, 'You know somethin', Horace? If it wasn't for that feller's moustache, I'd swear you was hirin' girls to tend your stock these days. I mean, ain't you got no regulations around here that say your men should get their hair cut regular?'

Hal and Tom were just about to start

braying again when Jack spun back around and fixed Walt with a steely look. 'Watch yourself, Devlin,' says he. 'I do not think you would care to feel my wrath.'

Walt's surprise lasted only a moment before it turned into rage. 'You threatenin' me, stock tender?' he roared. 'Is that it? You lookin' to start a fight?'

'I want no trouble from any of you,' Jack replied, tight-voiced. 'My only concern is for the welfare of the horse you just entrusted to me. I do not consider that to be a fighting matter, but I would not hesitate to fight a man among you who would try to fight *me*.'

'Then it looks like Hal was right about you after all,' said Walt. ''Pears you *are* a trouble-maker.' And so saying, he made to toss the contents of his glass into Jack's face.

But Jack dodged to one side, and as the whiskey went over his shoulder and splashed across the puncheon floor, he grabbed the hand holding the glass and rammed it straight back into Walt's contorted face.

The rim of the glass caught Walt in the mouth and shattered on impact, lacerating the hard, stubbly skin around his thick lips. Walt howled in surprise, and gave a little womanly shriek when he saw the blood begin to flow. Beside him, his brother mouthed a curse and went for his Colt, but again Jack was there before him, moving in quick to crowd him and thus restrict his movements, then tearing the weapon from his fingers and bringing it up sharply across his face.

By this time Walt was seeing red in more ways than one. With the roar of a bull buffalo he threw himself at Jack with his face twisted up into something furious, and his big, sausage-fingered hands hooked into talons.

Again Jack dodged to one side, as nimble as any prizefighter, and as Walt blundered past, he twisted around with him and cracked the barrel of Hal's Colt against his head.

It was lucky for Walt that his hat cushioned some of the blow, for I have seen many men cold-cocked in a moment of anger who never fully regained their faculties. Even with the dubious protection of his hat, however, the blow was still enough to send Walt crashing into, and then over, one of the tables. He struck the floor hard and yelped again, then started rolling around and moaning.

Tom Farson, suddenly looking straight down the muzzle of his brother-in-law's Colt, froze in the act of going for iron.

'A wise decision,' Jack complimented him. Without taking his eyes off the trio, he said, 'Mr Traylor. Take their guns, if you please.'

'Oh, now listen here, Jack–'

'*Do it,*' Jack hissed, and he had such a dominant character that Mr Traylor, who was to all intents and purposes *his* employer, actually jumped to do his bidding. He relieved Tom and Walt of their weapons and then, at Jack's command, emptied them.

'Bastard!' said Tom.

Jack ignored the insult. 'I meant what I said, gentlemen,' he reminded them. 'I neither want nor need trouble from you, but I can tell when a man goes out of his way to look for it, and I see that you are three such men. My advice to you is to quit while you're ahead. Do you hear me? Buy your supplies and get on back to your home range.'

'You'll pay for this!' promised Hal, nursing a gash in his cheek.

'Perhaps,' Jack answered with the faintest of smiles. 'But I doubt that you'll be the fellow to do the collecting.'

Tom Farson turned his attention to Mr Traylor, who by this time was looking a little ill. 'Is this was it comes to, Horace?' he snarled. 'You let your hired help bad-mouth us and then beat us up? Your best customers?'

'Give them back their weapons,' Jack said. 'And be warned, the three of you. Drop this business. It's not worth dying over.'

He unloaded Hal's Colt and, turning it around so that he was holding it by the barrel, thrust it towards its owner. Then he turned on his heel and strode out of there, left foot, right foot, left foot, right foot, slow and deliberate and completely in control of the situation.

Walt Devlin was finally winning his battle against unconsciousness. Slowly he clawed his way up onto his hands and knees. The wound at his mouth looked far worse than it was, but it still stung like a bitch. He grabbed the edge of the nearest table and hauled himself to his feet, muttering colourful curses under his breath, and sending out a sickly red spray from between his lips.

'I'll kill him!' he growled. 'Give me my gun! So help me, I'll kill him!'

Mr Traylor came forward and grabbed him by the shoulders to keep him right where he was. 'Don't be a fool, Walt!'

Walt shrugged him off. 'Get away from me! Just give me a gun and–'

'Walt! Walt, listen to me! *Listen!* I know you feel sore. Who wouldn't? But do you know who he is? That feller you want to start a shooting fight with?'

'I don't give a damn who he is! He's a

dead man, 'far as I'm concerned!'

Tom Farson must have picked up something in Mr Traylor's tone, because he came forward and said, 'Who is he then, Horace?'

Mr Traylor said, 'He's Jack Page, that's who he is. Jack *Page*.'

To hear him tell it afterwards, it went so quiet then that you could have heard a feather hit the floor boards, and the blood drained from each man's face as he realised just who it was he'd just tangled with. At last Hal Devlin said, *'The* Jack Page?', for even then he was regarded as something of a living legend by those who had heard of his exploits.

Mr Traylor nodded. *'The* Jack Page,' he confirmed. 'Now, cool down, you fellers. Cy, fetch these boys a refill. On the house. And bring the medicine chest; we got a couple of walking wounded to tend here.'

FOUR

To my complete surprise, Walt Devlin and the others followed Jack's advice to the letter; they bought their supplies, packed them aboard their mule and then rode out. But as I watched them go from my place at the common room window, I saw that Walt continued to push his limping horse just as hard as ever, and perhaps even more so. You could not tell that man anything, I thought with a shake of the head – and that's what made his peaceful retreat all the more remarkable.

We knew better than to believe that was an end to the matter, though. Walt Devlin would never let it go at that, not if he wanted to remain the biggest man in the county. But though we remained extra vigilant over the next couple of weeks, we saw neither hide nor hair of any Devlin or Devlin rider, so maybe we had been mistaken about him after all.

There was a subtle change in the general attitude towards Jack Page, however. Where before we had all been rather taken by his ready friendship and quick good humour, we now began to see something of the dark violence he kept contained within him. I have no doubt that Mr Traylor, Hetty and Cy Pollack grew to fear that long-haired, pale-faced man, and equally I am sure that Jack Page well knew he was the cause of their disquiet. But for my part, I continued to find myself drawn to him, and though he never really gave a good goddamn about the opinions of others, I flatter myself to think that he valued my continued friendship, such as it was, quite highly.

For his part, Jack seemed to forget all about the fight, and in his free moments he would saddle up his magnificent black horse and go riding. He would be missing for hours at a stretch, and I think there were times when Mr Traylor hoped he wouldn't come back at all, but eventually he always did.

On one occasion I watched him walk his horse in from the east and as he climbed down I took the reins from him. 'Good ride?' I asked.

He fingered his moustache. 'Most ... satisfactory,' he replied with a brief, secret smile.

'I swear, I've never known a-one for riding like you, Jack. You must love the countryside hereabouts.'

He shrugged. 'It is wild and isolated,' he said. 'But it has its ... compensations.'

I didn't know what he meant at the time, though later I found out in no uncertain terms.

Although nothing seemed to have come of his run-in with the men of the Lazy D, the fact remained that Jack had put Mr Traylor in an unenviable spot by involving him in the fracas that day, and Mr Traylor worried constantly about the prospect of encountering further trouble somewhere down the line. I heard him discussing it with Cy Pollack one day. He said it might still be possible to smooth things over with Walt – who was his best customer, after all – if Jack left the county. He had only been sent out to us in order to recover from his wounds, he said, and he had most certainly done that in the last couple of months, so there was really nothing to hold him there any longer. He did not relish the prospect of telling Jack that it would be best for all concerned if he moved on, but he resolved to do it that very afternoon.

Still, fate has a way of boxing-up even the best-laid plans, and its behaviour that day was no exception. Jack and I were in the cool brown shadows of the stable, harnessing up a fresh team for the afternoon stage to Franklin, when Mr Traylor appeared in the common room doorway and called out with studied casualness, 'Oh, Jack – could I have a word?'

Jack glanced at me across the broad back

of the horse. 'Can you finish this on your own, Ash?' he asked.

'Sure.'

I watched him leave the stable and cross the yard towards the station building. I had no idea how he would take being told he must leave, but I knew it wouldn't sit especially well with him, for he had never been a man to run away from confrontation, and would not do it willingly now.

He had almost reached Mr Traylor when suddenly the afternoon stage came careening around the low hills some distance out, moving at a far greater clip than was either safe or necessary. The coach came around the bend on two wheels; then, as the team straightened out to begin the homeward run, it crashed back down onto all four and began to rock perilously back and forth with its back end fishtailing wildly.

Leaving the fresh team part-harnessed, I hurried outside to watch the dramatic approach. I thought I could hear Jim Ballew, yelling something from his seat in the box, but it was difficult to be sure above the drum and thunder of the racing team and the rumbling drone of the speeding wheels.

I knew at once that something was very badly wrong, though. The horses were flecked with lather, wall-eyed and nearly spent. Jim would never push his team like that without good cause, and yet there he was, standing with his feet braced against the boards, his lines wrapped around one gloved hand and his whip in the other, flying and snapping over the heads of his straining animals like some peculiar airborne snake.

The coach continued slipping and sliding down the trail until at length Jim stamped on the brake and the crimson vehicle rocked to an ungainly halt before us, kicking up a cloud of dust around it.

'*Indians!*' yelled Jim, fairly hurling himself from the box. 'Indians, Horace! We was attacked!' He came around to the near-side door and tore it open. 'Here, give me a hand with Curly!'

'Was he hurt?' Mr Traylor asked worriedly.

'Arrow in the shoulder,' Jim replied frantically.

'Here,' said Jack, stepping forward. I watched as he and Jim Ballew wrestled Curly Thomas out of the coach. Curly was as white as a sheet. He was moaning and clutching his left shoulder with his right hand. The sky-blue shaft of the arrow was protruding from a patch of blood on his shirt that was shaped like a rose. They rushed him into the common room, leaving the five distraught passengers to push out of the coach after them and hustle into the building under their own steam.

I looked at the arrows projecting from the sides of the coach, and the splintery little holes where bullets had struck home. Anxiously I then scanned the trail, the hills, every patch of scrub and stand of trees, wondering if they were out there now, those Indians. But our surroundings were as peaceful as always.

I glanced over at the horses in the traces. They stood heads-down and heaving, their big, slab-like muscles still twitching and jumping. I knew the coach wouldn't be moving out again anytime soon, so I set about unhitching the team and turning them out into the corral, and tried not to hear the terrible screams of Curly Thomas as they fought to get the arrow out of him.

When at last I finally entered the common room, I saw that Mr Traylor was still struggling to calm the terrified passengers and Cy Pollack was halfway through cutting the head of the arrow out of Curly's shoulder. Jack Page was standing by one of the windows, turning the shaft of the arrow in his fingers and occasionally peering out into the surrounding countryside.

I went over to him and asked him what had happened.

'The coach was just fording March Creek,' he replied, naming a small tributary about five miles to the west, 'when a band of Cheyennes came out of nowhere and attacked it. Ballew was lucky; from that point on he's got about two miles worth of straight road ahead of him, so he was able to outrun them, but not before they wounded his shotgun guard and shook up the passengers.'

I peered around him at the man on the table. Curly Thomas was about my own age, nineteen going on twenty. Until that moment, I hadn't thought it possible that anyone so young could die, although of course it happened every minute of every day of every year. It was a sobering thought, and for the first time I began to consider my own mortality. 'Will he...' My voice dried up and I had to start again. 'Will he live, do you think?' I asked.

Jack glanced over his shoulder. 'Provided Cy knows what he's doing,' he replied. 'And no infection sets in.'

I turned my attention to the view beyond the window, trying to blot out the sounds Curly made writhing around on the puddled trestle table. 'I thought all the Indian trouble was confined to the northwest, anyway,' I said.

But in truth, I didn't know for sure. All I

knew was that when they weren't fighting each other, the Indians were fighting the whites, and often with good reason. This was at a time when the railroads were just beginning to work their way across the country, remember, and herd upon herd of buffalo was being decimated in order to feed the construction workers. And with the end of the War, thousands of soldiers were being sent back out to the west, and more troops inevitably meant more conflict.

Indeed, some of you may still remember the proud if foolish boast of Captain Fetterman, who said he could ride through the entire Sioux nation with just eighty men. Well, a young warrior name of Crazy Horse had killed him and exactly eighty men without even working up a sweat not six months past, and the tale was still being told around campfires right across the west.

'Do you think they'll attack us here?' I asked at length.

Jack shrugged. 'Possibly. We must certainly be a tempting target, having both whiskey and horses at our disposal.'

'Perhaps we should go armed, then,' I suggested. 'For a few days. You know, just in case.'

'Perhaps we should at that, Ash. Do you own a gun?'

'I have a Winchester.'

He raised one eyebrow, as well he might, for the rifle was barely a year old, and had cost me practically every cent I had. 'Then keep it handy,' he said. 'It could be that you'll get the chance to use it.'

Tense hours followed, as you might imagine, but finally the afternoon melted into early evening, and though we continued to go about our business with one eye on our shoulders, there was no further trouble. Cy Pollack removed the arrowhead from Curly's arm and bandaged him up, and we made a kind of pallet for him by the hearth, where he slept a deep feverish sleep. Likewise, we tried to make the temporarily stranded passengers as comfortable as we could, but they wanted only to continue on to the relative safety of Franklin, where they might forget this particular episode of their lives.

But Jim Ballew would not chance moving on again tonight. Quite apart from the possibility of another Indian attack, too much bouncing around might open up Curly's wound again. So like it or not, the passengers had to accept that they wouldn't be going anywhere before morning.

'Don't blame me, folks,' Jim protested over a meal that evening. 'This is Tall Bull's doin'. Him an' Roman Nose. Them two been agitatin' the whole Cheyenne nation for years.'

Mr Traylor saw the effect this line of conversation was having on the passengers, and tried to ease their fears as best he could. 'Now, come on, Jim. I'm sure Tall Bull's got more important matters to occupy him than the likes of us. Those braves you ran into today, they were likely just a party of high-spirited young bucks out to raise Ned. Nothing more sinister than that.'

Jim made a dismissive sound in his throat. 'You're welcome to your opinion, Horace.

71

But just you think about it a minute,' he continued. 'It's only been a couple years since them Cheyennes made life hell for the whites in these parts. Remember the trouble they caused, followin' that war they had with the Arapaho? An' Roman Nose, he's been stirrin' 'em up ever since Sand Creek.'

'Well, you can hardly blame him for that,' I said, speaking before I could stop myself.

Jim glared down the table at me. 'An' what's that supposed to mean?' he demanded.

I felt the eyes of everyone there upon me, and I coloured furiously, for I tended to get tongue-tied when speaking in company. I looked up at Jim and I wanted to tell him exactly what it was supposed to mean; that the Sand Creek Massacre was just that – a massacre. What else would you call the wanton slaying of an entire tribe by better than a thousand blood-hungry soldiers? Those men, women and children, largely unarmed, had thought they were in the protective custody of the very scum who had murdered them.

But somehow I could not argue the point. He was my elder, and I had always been taught to respect my elders. So all I said was, 'Nothing. It's ancient history now, anyway,' and I hated myself for backing down like that, when I knew I had as much right as anyone there to speak my piece.

I took a turn around the station at dusk, with my prized Yellow Boy rifle cradled in my arms. I had only ever used the weapon for hunting game. I couldn't imagine what it would be like to use it upon another human being, and hoped that I would never have to fid out. The evening was quiet but for the soughing of the wind in the trees, quiet and peaceful. But were those Cheyennes out there even at this moment, watching me from hiding? Ready to drive an arrow into me just as surely as they had driven one into Curly?

With a shiver I hustled back inside.

I was sure I would not sleep that night, but when I think back on it now, I cannot even remember my head hitting the pillow. I slept deep and dreamless, and the night grew several hours old, when suddenly a hand clamped firmly across my mouth.

I almost leapt from the mattress, but the hand holding me silent was strong, and so was its companion, when it suddenly gripped my left shoulder.

'Be quiet, Ash,' a voice whispered urgently. My heart was still thudding hard, but some of my initial panic began to subside, and now, as I squinted up through the darkness, I could just make out some of the features in the grey blur of the face hovering above me. The hand covering my mouth slipped away and I said, *'Jack!'*

'Not so loud,' he cautioned. 'They're out there, now. Creeping around the stable.'

I was still half-asleep. 'Who?' I asked, yawning.

'The Indians,' he whispered. 'I've been watching them. They're after the horses.' He straightened up, and I saw that he had put his Sharps rifle against the wall before wakening me. 'Get your Winchester, Ash.

It's time we went pot-hunting.'

I sat up and was about to do as he said when caution made me hesitate. 'Just the two of us?' I asked.

'Of course,' said he. 'We'll need the element of surprise if we're to catch them at it. How long do you think we'd go undetected with the others clumping about after us? Besides,' he added almost casually, 'there are only eight of them.'

'Eight!'

'Not so loud, I said!'

'But Jack ... two against eight ... it's madness.'

I just about saw the faint twisting of his moustache as a sour smile formed his lips. He inclined his head. 'Very well, Ash. As you wish. We'll just sit back and let them steal the horses.' As he made to turn away, he added over his shoulder, 'But I'm sorely disappointed in you, boy. I thought you had more sand.'

Before I properly knew what I was doing, I lunged out, grabbed him by the arm and spun him back to face me. I was so mad in that moment that I could have chewed nails and spat rust. Glaring at him, I said, 'Are you calling me a coward, damn you?'

His response was a sardonic lift of the eyebrow. 'Are you telling me that you're *not?*'

I could hardly believe my ears. I had thought he was my friend. Angrily I thrust him away from me and reached for my boots, glad that I had decided to go to bed fully-clothed this night. At last I snatched up my rifle and fixed him with a stern look. 'All right,' I hissed. 'Lead on.'

He did, and I followed. We left my small, spartan room, crept down to the back door and let ourselves out into the night. We were directly behind the store. I glanced up at the night sky. It was an immense oval bowl, purple velvet sprinkled with precious gems. I put the time at somewhere past midnight. It was bitterly cold, and I wished I had thought to don my jacket, as Jack had done, but if I am honest, I don't believe that was the only reason for my shivering.

I sensed movement close to me, and when I looked at Jack, I saw that he was waving me impatiently after him.

We light-footed it around the corner of the building and crouch-ran along the side of the dark store until we reached a spot from which we could view the stable on the other side of the yard. The night was absolutely quiet but for the odd snort and stamp of a fidgety horse. It seemed hard to believe that there were Cheyennes right on the doorstep, hard and frightening.

Jack turned to me. In the moon- and starlight, his thin face looked skeletal. His eyes and cheeks were just hollow pits, the skin around them a translucent grey. He whispered, 'They're around the far side of the stable.'

'What shall we do, then?'

He pointed off to the east. 'Go about thirty yards that way, then work your way around in a kind of half-circle, so that you come up on the corral from the side. Once you're in position, wait for my signal. Meanwhile, I'll approach them from the opposite direction, and if we're lucky we'll catch them in a cross-fire.'

Luck, I thought bleakly. *We'll be lucky if we just get through this business in one piece.* But I didn't say as much, I only nodded and broke cover, moving as quietly as I knew how, trying to move the way I had seen Jack himself move, so that I blended in with my surroundings, and thus became invisible.

I worked my way around towards the corral by the circuitous route Jack had described. It seemed to take an eternity. By the time I was within perhaps eighty feet of my destination, I was sweating like a pig. But now I could see them in the ghostly moon-glow – the Cheyennes.

I could not make out specifics, for the light was not that good, but it did appear that Jack's estimate of eight braves was correct. They must have left their own painted horses tethered back a-ways, and crept up to our lonely station from the south. There they had dismantled part of the pole fence, and now they were leading our horses out of the stable and off across the prairie, as calm as you like, stroking muzzles and whispering strange, guttural comfort-sounds to keep them quiet, and they were going docilely, for that is the way they had been trained.

I had to admire their gall, these Cheyennes, for the whole business was just as slick as butter, but at the same time I wanted to teach them a lesson – that *our* horses, above all others, were not for stealing.

I watched the Indians with a kind of morbid fascination, for I had not seen them often, and they were still a dangerous novelty to me. They were tall and rangy, by far the tallest Indians I had ever seen. Some of them wore blankets poncho-style and tied at the waist, it being so cold. Others wore rawhide leggings and fringed shirts decorated with lazy-stitch beadwork. I saw the glitter of their metal armbands when they moved, and tried to take note of their weaponry, which consisted mainly of old handguns and steel hatchets. A few of them carried what appeared to be rifles with cut-down barrels, while others had tomahawks – what they called tammixes – stuck in their belts. One of their number wore a magnificent warbonnet, though I was not sure if this necessarily made him a chief of any kind.

I realised that I was not so much gripping my rifle as strangling it, and forced myself to relax my grip. My palms were sweaty, and I wiped one after the other against my pants. It seemed that I had been hunkering behind this patch of scrub for hours, though I knew that could not be. But where was Jack? What was keeping him? He had told me to wait for his signal, whatever that might be, but the urge to do something to stop these Indians from stealing any more of our stock was growing stronger by the second.

Then, completely without warning, the deep, ominous crack of a long gun tore through the darkness and one of the Indians, just leading a horse through the gap in the fence, threw up his arms and screamed, and the horse reared up in fright, catching him with her forehooves and finishing what the bullet had started.

I crouched immobile for several seconds. I was shocked. I had never seen a man killed before. Then a second gunblast crashed through the night and another of them fairly flew backwards off his feet, and suddenly the Indians were fleeing, leaving the frightened horses they had been hoping to steal to mill in the corral, and all at once the darkness came to life with the sounds of men yelling and horses stamping and running, and the remorseless boom of Jack's powerful Sharps.

I realised with a start that one of the Cheyennes was racing straight towards me. It was the Indian in the warbonnet. I thought for a moment that he had seen me and was bent on attacking me. But then everything became clear. He was not so much running towards *me* as *away* from Jack.

Without pausing to consider the consequences, I came up and out from behind the scrub and he saw me across no more than thirty feet of open ground. He came to a slipping, sliding halt. I saw his face clearly; it was painted in black and yellow, with a lightning streak and several small white dots that were meant to denote hailstones.

Clearly he had been surprised to see me, but he recovered within seconds, maybe one second, and brought up an old Merwin & Hulbert, which he fired with a hideous scream.

I am sure I felt the wind of the bullet as it passed my face, though I know this cannot be so. I was too scared to do anything but fire my rifle once, then work the lever and fire once again, and I was lucky; the Cheyenne hunched up beneath the impact of the bullets and twisted around with an awful, gurgling cry, then fell to earth and bounced a little in the long, shushing grass.

Around me, small-arms fire crackled and popped. The retreating Indians were firing wildly into the night, not sure where their ambushers were, or how strong their number. I ignored it all. I felt sick, because I knew that in that moment I had killed my first man.

'Ash! Ash! Are you all right?'

Like a man coming out of a dream, I realised then that the Indians had gone, that the fight, such as it was, was over, and though my contribution to it had not been great, it had probably been the single most important act in the history of the world for the man I had killed.

I had trouble tearing my eyes away from the corpse I had made. I was trembling hard and my teeth were chattering. Then I heard the voice again. 'Ash? Are you–?'

'I'm here!' I called out. 'I'm all right!'

I went over to the body and, with some revulsion, toed it over onto its back. As near as I could estimate, the brave had been perhaps three or four years older than me. He had dark, staring eyes. His mouth was open. One rotting tooth marred an otherwise pristine ivory flash. My first bullet had ripped into his left breast, just above the nipple. My second had made an awful, scrambled mess of his stomach.

Jack came jogging out of the night, the still-smoking Sharps held slantwise across his chest. He glanced down at the body at my feet and said, 'Good work, Ash. Between us, we killed three of them, and I'm sure I wounded one more.'

We heard some sounds coming from the station. The women were screaming, the men only now venturing out to yell confused questions. Jack raised his voice and told them to calm down, that we'd just stopped the Indians from stealing our horses. He made it all sound so ordinary, as if it were a matter of little note, something we might have done every night at that hour. Then he looked down at me and, after a moment, put his free hand on my shoulder.

'Feel sick?' he asked gently.

I nodded. 'A little.'

'It'll pass,' he said. 'You've gone from a boy to a man tonight, Ash. That's a big step. But it's a man you are, now. And one of the things that being a man means is that you can never back down from anyone ever again, the way you did with Jim Ballew earlier tonight.' He paused a moment, watching my face to make sure I understood properly what he meant, and then he began to stride back towards the corral, where the horses would need tending.

'Oh, and by the way,' he said, turning back when he was about a dozen feet away. 'You didn't *really* think I doubted your courage, did you?'

I looked at him, that skeleton in the darkness, and thought about it. 'I don't know,' I mumbled honestly.

'Well, for what it's worth, Ash, I'd say you've got sand a-plenty, and a sight more than most.'

It was high praise indeed, and it made me feel warm and proud to hear it, but it did not change the fact that I had made not one but *two* transitions during that fight. I had gone from a boy to a man, certainly, but I had also gone from a man to a killer.

I resolved there and then that I would never kill another man as long as I lived, and

I meant it, too. But as I have already noted, fate has a way of boxing up even the best-laid plans, and on that day, and all the subsequent days of my life, its behaviour was no exception.

FIVE

The stranded passengers left for Franklin at first light the following morning, and since Curly was still in no position to be moved around much, Jack volunteered to act as shotgun guard for the remainder of the journey. The rest of us watched them rock and sway off down the trail, leaving a cloud of dust in their wake, and offered up a little prayer that they would get through in one piece, then got on with our chores.

But as I made myself busy, I began to think about what had happened, *really* happened, the previous night, and to understand that I had indeed reached a turning point in my life. The admiration with which we had been greeted upon our return from the stable had taken me completely by surprise. Mr Traylor, Cy Pollack, Hetty – they had all hailed us as heroes for seeing off the red menace, and though Jack was already quite used to such adulation, it was still very new to me. For the first time I began to get a sense of self-worth, to appreciate that I was more than just a lowly stablehand, and though it shames me to admit it now, that feeling went a considerable way towards swamping the guilt I felt over killing the Indian. Oh, and in case you were wondering – though he had worn a warbonnet, he was not a chief. The way Jack explained it to me later, the dead buck was probably a warrior who had proven his courage in some earlier battle, and wore his bonnet now as a symbol of his valour. The Cheyennes were like that. So at least I had the distinction of having killed a proven warrior, if nothing else.

And, whilst we're clearing up a few loose ends, I don't know whatever happened to Mr Traylor's intention to tell Jack to leave. My feeling is that, after that business with the Indians, he realised that Jack was a valuable man to keep just where he was.

For their part, however, the Cheyennes were unbowed by their defeat that night, and over the next few weeks we heard of further depredations in our neck of the woods. The most infamous of these, and the one that usually finds its way into most history books, concerns their attack upon a stagecoach going west. They hit it about four miles out from our station, and the driver, Tom Pascoe, was killed along with three of the passengers – and all so that they could steal the six-horse team. It was because of this outrage, in fact, that the Overland decided to temporarily suspend all operations in the area.

Things became a little strained around the station, what with the constant threat of Indian attack, but there were always chores to do, and so we contrived to find comfort in good honest toil. Only Jack seemed able to carry on as normal, and whenever the opportunity arose, he would saddle up his big black horse and go riding for hours at a time, heedless of the possible danger.

About three weeks after our run-in with the Indians, Cy Pollack spotted a bunch of riders coming in from the northwest and promptly raised the alarm. In next to no time we all came running with our guns at the ready, but by then the figures were beginning to take on shape and form, and it was with some relief that we were able to identify them as a detachment of mounted soldiers.

Twenty minutes later they rode into the yard, twelve of them, two abreast, with a lieutenant at their head and a black-bearded sergeant sitting in his saddle wearily right behind him. The lieutenant signalled for his detachment to halt about twenty yards out, then he and his NCO walked their chestnut horses towards us and the lieutenant lifted one gauntleted hand in a casual salute.

'Good morning,' he said. He was about twenty-two or three, clean-shaven and tanned, with blond hair and blue eyes. His uniform, like those of his men, was creased and travel-stained and far too hot and impractical for the hard riding they appeared to have been doing. 'Lieutenant Arthur Gregson, out of Camp Lee, at your orders. This is Sergeant Rawlings. Would you happen to have a Mr Traylor among you, by any chance?'

Mr Traylor nodded. 'I'm Traylor,' he said, reaching up his hand. 'Pleased to meet you, lieutenant. Would you care to light and set a spell? We'd be happy to supply coffee for your men.'

Gregson nodded. 'Thank you, Mr Traylor, we'd appreciate that.' He twisted around in his McClellan saddle and gave orders for his men to see to the comfort of their mounts, then he dismounted, handed his reins to the sergeant and followed us all into the common room, his sheathed sabre bumping softly against his hip as he moved.

It was a warm day, as I recall, and the temperature inside the common room was only marginally cooler than outdoors. The little windows were squares of pure white light, and it was hard to discern anything beyond them because the sky was so bright. Flies flew in triangles and oblongs up around the low ceiling. Their buzzing increased as we clattered into the room.

We sat at the trestle table and Hetty went to fetch coffee. Gregson took off his forage cap and tossed it onto the bench beside him, then loosened his uncomfortable stand-up collar. His face was streaked with sweat and his eyes looked dark and hollow, deprived of sleep.

'We've been after these bloody-hand Cheyennes you've had trouble with just lately,' he explained. 'Seems they made things too hot for themselves up in the Powder River country and decided to try their luck in pastures new. Here.'

'We heard they'd been raiding the Lazy D,' Cy Pollack replied.

Gregson nodded briskly. 'Stealing horses and killing cattle,' he confirmed. 'Then, of course, there was the business of that stagecoach they attacked.'

'A tragedy,' said Mr Traylor. 'And right on our doorstep, too.'

'The word is that you had a run-in with them yourselves, a while back.'

'Sure did,' said Mr Traylor. 'Before they did for old Tom Pascoe, they attacked one of our coaches and wounded the shotgun guard. The same night, they tried to steal our horses, but my two hired men here were too sharp for 'em. Killed three and sent the rest packing.'

Lieutenant Gregson appraised Jack and me with interest. 'That's about what I was told. I'm also told that one of you is Jack Page.'

'I'm Page,' Jack said with a nod.

'Then you're the man I've really swung by to see, Mr Page.'

'Oh?'

'Yes, sir. To ask for your help.'

Hetty arrived with a tray laden with steaming mugs. We all made thank-you sounds or gestures, and as she hustled away to see about the soldiers outside, Gregson continued. 'We've been chasing these Cheyennes around in circles for about five days now, Mr Page. But they're too slick for us. They hit hard and they hit fast, but then they vanish, and so far we haven't been able to track them down.' He paused and reached for his mug. 'I think we'd do a lot better if we had someone with us who savvied Indians.'

'Meaning me?'

'You have had some experience with them, I understand?'

'Some,' Jack allowed, and I believe that was the closest he ever came to confirming that story about him being a squaw man.

Gregson said, 'May I speak frankly, Mr Page?'

'It's the only way *to* speak, lieutenant.'

Gregson seemed to agree with that. 'Very well. Did you take a look at the men in my command? Enlisted men from back East.

Ohio, Pennsylvania, New York. They haven't been out here much more than a month. What do they know about this country, or Indians, or Indian-fighting? And my own experience is hardly more inspiring. We need a man who knows what he's about. Someone who can help us track these Cheyennes to their camp and lend a hand if it comes to a fight.'

Jack considered for a moment. I think Gregson's request appealed to his vanity. At length he said, 'Do you think you could spare me for a few days, Mr Traylor?'

The station manager gestured with his chubby little hands. 'If you're game for it, Jack,' he said. 'If it'll help the army capture these renegades.'

Jack nodded decisively. 'All right, then, lieutenant. You've got yourself a scout. But you do *what* I say, *when* I say. Do you understand?'

Gregson inclined his head. 'Naturally, I will defer to your greater experience.'

Satisfied, Jack turned to regard me. 'Care

to come along for the exercise, Ash?' he asked, taking me completely by surprise with the invitation.

I looked from him to Mr Traylor and muttered, 'Well … I don't… I mean…'

'You've got nothing better to do around here until the line starts operating again,' he pointed out. 'And the line won't start operating until these Indians are captured or killed.'

That was true enough. But I still wasn't totally sure I was cut out for such an adventurous – not to mention dangerous – life. 'Well, if Mr Traylor can spare me…' I began uncertainly, hoping that he couldn't.

Without waiting for an answer, Jack reached over and clapped me on the arm. 'Good. That's settled.'

'Where do we begin then, Mr Page?' asked the lieutenant.

Jack must have already pondered that, for his answer came quickly. 'With a trap,' he replied. 'This is a vast country. The Cheyennes could be hiding out anywhere. So we need something to lure them out into the open.'

Gregson frowned. 'I'm not sure I follow you, sir.'

'If we're going to set a trap, lieutenant, we'll need bait. Something the Indians will find impossible to resist.' He thought for a moment, then smiled. 'A stagecoach,' he said.

Mr Traylor was clearly puzzled. 'A stagecoach, Jack?'

'Yes. They've already attacked two. Let's see if we can't make it third time *un*lucky.'

'But the route's been suspended–'

'Then we must have it opened up again,' Jack declared theatrically. 'And when we send the first coach out from Franklin, we must make sure it is drawn by six of the finest horses in the entire Overland cavvy.'

At last comprehension dawned in Gregson's tired eyes. 'I think I see what you're driving at, Mr Page. The Overland company sends out a stage – the bait – and we follow on at a safe distance, ready to surprise the

Indians when they attack it.'

Jack shook his head. 'Almost, lieutenant. But not quite. The coach will lure the Cheyennes out certainly. But maybe not all of them. So we rely on a few of your men, posing as passengers, to fight them off. Then *we* follow them, right the way to their camp, and ensure that we catch the entire band.'

Gregson positively beamed. 'It sounds fine in principle, Page. But there are no guarantees. It *could* go wrong.'

'If it looks as if it's about to go wrong, we'll take a hand in the fight ourselves. If not, we'll hold back and stick to our original plan.'

'Do you think you can get the Overland to go along with you?'

Jack said, 'I would say they'd do almost anything to get this route opened up again. Every day it remains closed costs them a fortune.'

'Very good, Mr Page. I'll be honest with you. I can think of no better plan. And I don't believe my superiors are so much concerned about *how* I get results, just as long as I *do* get them. So we'll give it a whirl.'

Later, Jack and I saddled up and prepared to move out with the soldiers. I owned a rather scraggy, dun-coloured mustang and an old three-quarter rig. Next to Jack, with his fine Tennessee thoroughbred and beech-made saddle, with its leather seat over a rawhide cover, I looked very poor indeed. As we tightened cinch-straps, Jack said, 'We'll have to get you a handgun, Ash. Long guns are all well and good when you're a-foot, but when you're astride a running horse, you need something smaller.'

I remembered something I had noticed during our run-in with the Cheyennes. 'Is that why the Indians cut down their rifle-barrels, then? Because they do most of their fighting from horseback?'

He laughed and nodded. 'Indeed it is, Ash. Indeed it is.' Then he fixed me with a look and said, 'You're learning, aren't you?'

We led our horses out into the sunshine. Gregson's sergeant, Rawlings, was just giving the order to mount up. As we also swung across leather, I studied the soldiers from beneath the shade of my hat-brim. They were, as Gregson had commented, a woefully inexperienced bunch. I should put their average age at about twenty, twenty-one, although a couple were older and at least three were considerably younger. They had doubtless been carpenters, con men, ferrymen and miners before joining up, but I doubted that even one of them had ever soldiered before. You only had to watch the awkward way in which they mounted up to see that they were not natural horsemen. Neither was their weaponry much better. I did not know much more about firearms than any other man, but I knew enough to recognise antiques when I saw them, and I saw them on those men, from their Cooke Brothers' and Merrill carbines to their long-barrelled, converted Colts.

Gregson climbed across leather and we

rode out, he and Jack at the head of our column, the somewhat taciturn Sergeant Rawlings and I next in line. Soon we left the station behind us and followed the trail east, through the rolling, hilly country towards Franklin.

Franklin lay about twenty miles away. It was a sizeable town of mostly tarpaper, log and board construction, and it derived the overwhelming bulk of its commerce from the surrounding ranches and farms. We arrived within sight of the place sometime around late afternoon and at the lieutenant's command, set about bivouacking on high ground about a quarter of a mile outside the town limits. I knew that it was Jack's intention to ride into town with Gregson and see the manager of the Overland office there to oh-so-casually arrange to 'borrow' a stagecoach and six, but I did not dream that he would want me to go with him.

'In case you had forgotten, we have business in town, you and I,' he said when I made to go and join the enlisted men.

Business? I did not get into town that much, and to be honest, I never really cared to. I did not like to be around large numbers of people any more than I could help. It was not that I had anything against them. It was just that I was at my happiest with my own company. But I had learned long before that you did not argue with Jack Page, and so I rode into town with them.

I bought myself a meal at a nearby eatery while Jack and the lieutenant went to conduct their business. I never did find out if the company raised any objections to Jack's plan, but I suspect that if they did, Jack soon talked them round. He nearly always did. All I did know was that when he joined me at the restaurant thirty minutes later, everything had been arranged.

'And that's not all, Ash,' he said, sitting across from me. 'Jim Ballew has been volunteered to drive the rig for us.'

Now that *was* a turn-up. Though he was a sociable enough fellow when the mood was upon him, I had long felt that Jim was what we used to call long on talk and short on guts. Now perhaps we would find out if I was right. 'I bet he was thrilled by the prospect,' I remarked drily.

'He was like a puppy with two tails,' Jack agreed with a hearty laugh. 'Now, eat up, Ash. We have some shopping to do.'

I frowned. 'Shopping?'

'We've got to get you properly armed for this campaign.'

I objected at once. 'I can't afford a pistol, Jack–'

'*I* can,' he said.

'I can't take your charity.'

He feigned surprise. 'Did I say anything about charity?' he asked. 'You can pay me back when you have some money in your pockets.'

He took me along to Sweeny's Gun Store on First and selected an Adams .442, which he handed to me butt-first. 'How does it feel?' he asked.

I hefted it. 'Heavy.'

'But comfortable? How does it fit your palm?'

I tried to get the feel of it. 'It fits well enough,' I said after a moment.

'And the balance?'

'I've got to be honest with you, Jack. I don't even know what it is I'm supposed to be looking out for.'

He smiled at me. 'It will come in time,' he predicted. 'You'll know when a weapon feels just right.'

We took some shells and went out into the rear yard, which had been set up for target practice. 'Now, be careful,' Jack instructed. 'This gun has a double action. Do you understand what I mean?'

'You mean I don't have to cock it before I fire it,' I replied, slightly irritated that he should treat me as a complete novice. 'I just pull the trigger.'

'*Squeeze* the trigger,' he corrected.

I loosed off a few shots and missed the target practically every time, but under his patient tutelage I began to grow more used to the weight and feel of the piece, and after twenty minutes, I actually hit the target twice, albeit far from centre.

'Do you think it is the gun for you?' Jack asked as we re-entered the store.

I looked at it. 'Well, I guess so. But–'

'Then we'll take it, Mr Sweeny,' he said. 'And a gunbelt as well.'

That night we slept under the stars, and as I lay in my blanket, I wondered what the morrow would bring. A confrontation with the Cheyennes, if we were lucky. *If we were lucky.* I had to smile at that. I thought about Jim Ballew. Long on talk and short on guts, I had told myself. But was I so very different? What man in his right mind ever really enjoyed dicing with death?

Turning my head, I glanced over at Jack's sleeping form, a few yards away. Here was such a one, I told myself.

I wanted to be like him very much, to do all the things he had done and command the same level of respect from everyone I met, but I knew I had neither the confidence *nor* the courage.

I was scared. The prospect of locking horns with the Indians once again terrified me, for I did not want to die, did not even want to suffer the slightest of wounds at their hands.

There. I had admitted it at last, if only to myself. But the confession made me feel no easier, and I went to sleep that night praying that, when the time came, I would not let Jack down.

Dawn came all too soon, and we were up just as the first watery grey streamers began to spread their long fingers out across the dark sky. We breakfasted on beef hash and dry bread washed down by black, sour-tasting coffee. I had heard that army cooks killed more soldiers than the Indians, and I could well believe it.

I watched Jack move among the men, instilling discipline where Gregson and his NCO seemed to have failed. He looked resplendent in his broad-brimmed sombrero and black frock coat, his bright red sash and matched Remingtons. Shortly thereafter we broke camp, saddled up and rode into town.

A coach was all ready and waiting for us out in front of the Overland office, and six of the sleekest black thoroughbreds I had ever clapped eyes on stood patiently in the traces. This was indeed a target the Indians would find difficult to resist.

We reined down outside the office. Around us the town was only just starting to wake up. Four of the enlisted men were assigned to travel inside the coach as passengers, and Sergeant Rawlings, having tried his best to look more like a civilian than a soldier, was given the unenviable task of riding up on the seat with Jim Ballew. It had already been agreed that the remainder of the column would follow on at a safe distance, maybe half a mile or a bit more.

Jack, Lieutenant Gregson and I dismounted, looped our reins over the tie rack and went into the office. The weight of the gun at my hip still felt strange, but not especially uncomfortable. Jim Ballew was sitting on a bench just this side of a neat mahogany fence that bisected the office, leaning forward slightly and hugging himself. Jack looked from him to Murray Stein, the Overland manager, who was pacing backwards and forwards in front of his desk in the corner.

Jack sensed his agitation at once. 'What is it?' he asked.

Murray was a big-bellied man with heavy Jewish features, a dark complexion and thinning black hair. He was in his early forties. 'Jim's been taken sick,' he replied.

All eyes fell to Jim Ballew, who looked back at us with an expression of acute misery and hugged himself some more. 'I got the stummick cramps,' he moaned. 'They's no way I can tool that coach along feelin' the way I do.' He assumed a look of profound regret as he added, 'Much as I'd like to.'

'Can you scare up another driver, Mr Stein?' asked the lieutenant.

'Not easily. Ever since we suspended operations, they've been deployed elsewhere. I could maybe find you one by this afternoon.'

'Are you sure you're too ill to drive the coach for us?' Jack asked.

Jim Ballew moaned some more. 'Sure I'm sure. I'm dyin', Page. It was the mutton broth I had across at Murphy's place last night. Meat must'a been on the turn.'

'I had the mutton broth at Murphy's last night,' I said. 'I'm all right.'

'I had two helpin's,' Jim replied testily. 'That was my undoin'.'

'You better get along home, then, Jim,' Murray said, coming through the little gate. 'I'll drive the coach myself.' He looked a little sick at having volunteered for the job, as well he might. He was a married man with five young children. Jim Ballew only had himself to worry about, and every man there knew he was feigning his sickness, just as sure as night follows day.

'You, Murray?' croaked Jim. I guess he felt he had to make a token protest at least, just to make himself appear more convincing.

'But you got your work here.'

'If it'll help nail these savages and get the route opened up again…' Murray said with a shrug.

'All right, Mr Stein,' Jack said with a nod. 'We appreciate your help.' He fixed Jim with a hard look, but when he spoke, his voice was surprisingly gentle. 'Come on, Jim, let me give you a hand there.' And he went over, put an arm around Jim's shoulders and helped him out of the door.

What happened out there I cannot say, but sure as hell something did. As the door closed behind them, Murray gave a nervy little laugh and said, 'You know, it's been so long since I drove a coach, I hope I haven't forgotten how it's done.'

He pushed back through the gate and went over to the hat rack to get his jacket. It was just as he started to reach up that the door swung open again and Jim Ballew re-entered the room. This time he really *did* look sick. 'Stay where you are, Murray,' he said after clearing his throat. 'I … I feel some better now. I'll make the run.'

Murray looked at him, puzzled. Just a moment ago, he'd been at death's door. 'You sure, Jim?'

'Yeah, I ... I'm sure.'

We followed Jim out onto the boardwalk. Jack had already mounted up and was waiting by the tie rack. I saw Jim glare at him before climbing up onto the seat. I stepped up to the saddle beside Jack, and he muttered, 'I've got no time for a man who shirks his responsibilities. Have you, Ash?'

I shook my head. 'No. Is that what you told Jim, to make him have a change of heart?'

He shrugged. 'Plain speaking never hurt anyone,' he opined. 'And if you question his manhood, a fellow will usually rise to the bait and try to prove you wrong.' He finally turned to regard me. 'Sometimes you have to make a man more afraid to say no than to say yes, if you're to get anywhere in this life.'

I pondered that. It was true, like so much of what he said. But was it right to goad and challenge and threaten a man in order to get him to do your bidding? I thought not, but I refrained from comment, for I was one of those men who were more afraid to say no than yes.

With the four enlisted men safely installed in the coach and Sergeant Rawlings up in the box, Jim cracked his whip over the heads of the team and the coach gave a jerk and started on its way at a steady walk. Gregson and the rest of us watched it go. It could be that this business today would be a waste of time. Part of me hoped that indeed it would. But at the same time, I knew I could not shirk my responsibilities any more than Jim had tried to shirk his. In which case, the sooner I faced the Indians again and over-came my fear – the better.

SIX

Jim held his team to a walk right the way down to the end of First. Then, as the road gave way to the rutted trail, he cracked his whip some more and with another lurch the coach began to pick up speed. By this time, the day was growing up and the sky was transforming itself into a clear delft blue. We waited there outside the Overland office and willed the time to pass. The stagecoach vanished in a cloud of dust, and we watched the dust slowly settle. Finally a quarter of an hour went by, and at a nod from Jack, Gregson gave the command to mount up and move out.

The land stretched out around us, ridged and green and bordered by far grey peaks. Those peaks, the foothills of the Rocky Mountains, had been seamed and shaped by the winds and rains of a million years. The stagecoach had long since been lost to sight beyond the low, timbered hills, but every so often we saw it as a crimson-and-saffron splash against the aquamarine swells.

We rode in silence but for the creak of leather, the jangle of accoutrements and the tattoo of horse-hoofs against hard-packed dirt. The morning wore along and warmed up. Sweat darkened my shirt at armpits and back. Far away to our right I spied a small stone cottage with a corral and outbuilding. That was Kate Spickett's place. I knew very little about her, save that she was Walt Devlin's woman, and that she had an independent streak. Certainly she would need to be a bold individualist to live right the way out here all by herself. I did not know where she had come from or why she had come to live out here away from most other folks. Perhaps she was someone after my own heart, but more likely Devlin, who was a fiercely jealous man, preferred to keep her isolated until she finally succumbed to one of his many proposals of marriage.

In the opposite direction I could just about discern tiny white-brown shapes dotting the distant pastures. They would be some of Devlin's grazing Herefords.

We rode on. I estimated that we were no more than perhaps eight miles from the Snake River station now, approaching a stretch of the road that snaked around low, wooded hills before opening out into a flat, straight run. If some Cheyenne scout had spotted the stage and he and his friends had decided to hit it, they would do it soon. The land directly ahead offered good cover for an attacking force. The stage had to slow speed considerably to negotiate all the bends safely. And if they wanted to make sure they got their hands on those six fine horses, they would have to strike before the team could be changed at the station.

The trail continued to unwind beneath us like a strip of brown corduroy. I glanced over at Jack. He was riding straight-backed and stern-faced. I do not know what was going through his mind in those moments, but I felt sure that he was thinking the same thing as me; that it was here in this section of winding hill country that Tom Pascoe's coach had been raised, and Tom himself killed.

Then, completely without warning, we heard it. A gunshot, followed by another; another; a whole fusillade, popping and cracking in the distance like firecrackers at Thanksgiving.

Jack raised one hand and we drew rein. Some of the enlisted men began to haul their carbines from leather. They knew the plan, that we would not get involved if we could help it, but they were acting on instinct. I glanced around at them and saw with some small measure of consolation that they looked just as scared-stiff as me. Beneath us, sensing our sudden excitement, our horses began to sidestep and toss their heads and blow air out through their distended nostrils. As we worked to get them back under control, Jack turned to the lieutenant and said,

'I'll go out ahead and see what's happened. If I think your men need assistance, I'll fire three shots in rapid succession. All right?'

Gregson bobbed his head. 'Right.'

Jack gave his black horse its head and the animal tore off up the trail and disappeared around the shoulder of a low, brushy hill, leaving the rest of us with the hardest job of all – just waiting.

All the while, gunfire had continued to sound. I might have been mistaken, but I thought I heard the high, wild yapping of excited braves mixed in with it as well. We held our horses as steady as we could, unable to do anything but listen.

It went on for about five minutes, if that, but of course, in retrospect it seemed to us as if it went on for much longer. Then the gunfire began to grow more patchy, and soon it decreased still further to just the odd single, echoing crack.

Still we held our horses where they were, just waiting, and hating the waiting. I did not care for the silence that took over from the sounds of combat, for at least while you could hear gunfire you knew within a little what was happening.

I saw the lieutenant stiffen beside me, and when I followed his line of vision, I saw why. Jack had just appeared around the bend in the trail about fifty yards ahead, and as he reined in, his horse reared up on its hind legs and pawed at the air. Jack himself waved us on, then turned his animal and galloped back the way he'd come.

This we did. The horses beneath us could hardly wait to get moving again and we had a hard time trying to hold them to a safe run. We rounded the bend in the trail, came to another, and another. Low hills shelved up on either side to hem us in. We continued to follow the road until at last the land began to open up and flatten out again.

At length we spotted the stagecoach. It was stalled slantwise across the trail, and the team was stamping and shifting in the traces, clearly anxious to get away from this place of man-made thunder and man-made violence.

Jim Ballew, Rawlings and the four enlisted men were standing beside the vehicle. One of the men was clutching his blood-stained arm, and another was inspecting the wound. The rest were still holding their guns at the ready, in case the departed Cheyennes decided to come back. Of Jack there was no sign.

We reined down in a cloud of dust. About thirty yards out lay two brown warriors. I could tell from the grotesque, unnatural way in which they were sprawled that they were dead. A painted Indian pony was down on its side some way off, struggling vainly to rise. It looked frightened, and there was blood on its heaving flank. Everywhere I looked I saw discarded sky-blue arrows, the odd lance projecting at an angle from the ground.

'Report, sergeant,' Gregson barked as he dismounted.

Rawlings spat. 'They attacked us, jus' like Page figured they would, 'bout an even dozen of 'em. We returned fire, killed two, wounded maybe as many again. Then they rode off to the north. Page lit out after 'em to chase up some sign.'

Gregson glanced that way. I could tell he was anxious to continue the chase. Doubtless he saw some possibility of promotion in this affair, if it all went according to plan. He glanced across at the wounded man, who was sitting in the stagecoach doorway, cursing. 'This your only casualty, sergeant?'

'Sir. Private Garrity. The In'ians winged 'im.' He scratched at his black beard. 'He'll be all right, just as soon as we get a tourniquet around his arm to stop the bleedin'.'

'See to it,' said Gregson. At last he turned his attention to Jim who was leaning against the off-side front wheel, ashen-faced. 'Thank you for your help, Mr Ballew. You did a good job. You can turn this rig around and head back to Franklin now.'

'You don't need to tell me twice,' Jim grunted.

'I'd be grateful if you could take my wounded man back with you. Sergeant –

detail one of the men to go with him and make sure he gets proper medical assistance.'

'Sir!'

I could hardly bear to hear the terrible, scared sounds the dying horse was making, but no one else seemed to care much or take any notice. I looked across at the animal. It seemed to look right back at me as it fought to rise up. There was confusion in its big dark eyes. It did not know what had happened to it, only that it did not want to carry on hurting like it was now.

I dismounted and tied my mustang to some brush. I didn't want to do what I was going to do, but neither could I stand by and watch the creature suffer any longer. I went over to it, tight in the throat, hardly able to breathe, and took out my brand new revolver. The horse looked up at me. I swallowed noisily, licked my lips, took aim and shot it in the head. It jerked once, as if in surprise, and its legs stiffened out. I closed my eyes then, and struggled hard not to be sick. When I opened my eyes again, my vision was blurred with hot tears, which I hurriedly blinked away.

As I returned to my mount, Jack rode down from the north to rejoin us. 'Get your men ready to press on, lieutenant,' he said. 'They're leaving a trail even a blind man could follow.'

'To horse, men!' cried Gregson.

I needed no second bidding, for by throwing myself into the chase, I hoped to exercise the image of that poor dying horse from my mind. Rawlings and the two enlisted men not returning to town with Jim Ballew also hurried to the saddle, for we had fetched their mounts out with us.

As I settled myself more comfortably, I felt Jack's glittering blue eyes upon me, and when I looked over at him, I saw that he was frowning. 'Are you all right, Ash?' He asked quietly, so as not to embarrass me before the other men.

I nodded. 'Yes. Come on, let's ride.'

We did. Jack led us up the slope and into a

patch of more broken country, all hill and hollow, with some timber, though not much, and craggy blue mountains soaring skyward against the horizon. This was an endless expanse of porcupine grass and bluestem, of blanketflowers and butterweeds. Gregson heeled his chestnut up alongside us and with one hand clapped atop his kepi to stop it blowing off in the slipstream, called across, 'Where does this lead to, Mr Page?'

Jack replied, 'The border. Dakota Territory lies that way, about fifteen miles or so.'

'Do you think that's where the Cheyennes are hiding out?'

'I don't know. Perhaps. The Black Hills are over to the north and west. They could lose themselves well enough in the foothills there. Then again, the badlands are directly ahead of us. We'd have the devil's own job tracking them in country like that.'

But that was for the future. At the moment the Indians had left tracks enough for us to follow with ease, and they stretched as a wide band of churned-up earth across one gentle swell after another.

We rode on for a couple of miles, and then the land flattened out and we reined our horses to a stand as we came to the sluggish waters of the Snake River. It was plain to see that the Cheyennes had swum their horses across to the far bank and then continued their retreat north. We could tell by the current that the river ran relatively shallow here, so it should present little problem to make a crossing of our own. One by one, we walked our horses down the reedy bank and into the cool water, and then held onto saddlehorn and mane while the horses did all the work getting us to the far side.

We followed the tracks for another hour, until we came upon a dead Cheyenne in the horse-belly-high grass. Then Jack signalled a halt and swung down to inspect the body, leaving his horse ground-hitched. Around us, the afternoon was beginning to wane, and grey cloud was bubbling up from the west.

The dead man lay on his back, bare-chested, his crotch barely covered by his breechclout. Flies had already gathered to fest upon the exposed meat of the gunshot wound in his stomach.

After a while Jack came back and mounted up. If he was as revolted by the spectacle as the rest of us he did not let it show. 'One of the braves your men wounded in the fray,' he said, confirming what we had already guessed. 'He must have held on for as long as he could, but in the end his heart gave out. Damn.'

'What?'

Jack looked at the lieutenant. 'One of the things you will learn about the Cheyennes if you stay out here for any length of time,' he replied, 'is that they are great mourners who honour their dead for days afterward.' He indicated the corpse. 'And yet they left this fellow where he fell.'

Gregson's frown was clear in his voice. 'What are you getting at?'

'That they knew, or guessed, that they were being pursued.'

'Impossible! We stayed far back out of sight the whole morning!'

Jack shrugged. 'If they spotted the coach, they could just as easily have spotted us.'

'Then why *attack* the coach, if they knew it was a trap?'

'I didn't say for sure that they *did* know. Perhaps it only occurred to them after your men began to fight back.'

'Damn! Then they could go to ground anywhere.'

Jack scanned our bleak, remote surroundings. 'Yes,' he agreed thoughtfully. 'They could. Or they could have drawn us out here deliberately, to get their own back.'

'Do you think they could do that?'

'If there's enough of them.'

Gregson clearly did not like the sound of that, and I couldn't blame him, for just the prospect of it sent a thrill of ice from the nape of my neck down to the base of my spine. The lieutenant looked around uneasily. Behind us, I heard his men doing likewise. 'What ... what do you suggest, then,

Page?' he asked at last.

Jack took out and checked his turnip watch. The long day was dying. 'If they want a fight,' he said, 'we'll oblige them.'

'I'd as lief know the strength of the enemy before I tangle with it.'

'You will, lieutenant,' Jack replied calmly. 'You will.' He pointed to a patch of high ground about a quarter of a mile away that was sheltered from the rising wind by a stand of rather scrubby oak and scattered rocks. 'It's too risky to go on now,' he said, 'especially if the Cheyennes *do* know we're after them. We'll camp up there for tonight.'

'Will we be safe?'

'I should think so.'

'The Cheyennes won't try to come at us under cover of darkness?'

'They do not fight at night.'

'They attacked your *station* at night.'

'That was different,' Jack replied with a glance at me. 'They came to steal horses, not fight. No, lieutenant. They will spend this evening mourning their dead, and attack us at first light tomorrow.'

'And what do you suggest we do about *that?*'

Jack fingered his moustache and smiled grimly. 'Oh, I'm sure we will think of something.'

He angled his mount off towards the camp-site he had indicated, and we followed after him. He had chosen the spot well, and the profusion of craggy rocks and mossy deadfalls gave the grove a comforting air of security, although the trees still standing were twisted, tormented-looking things that seemed intent on gouging out the dark underbellies of the clouds gathering above us. We dismounted in the grassy clearing at the rough centre of the arbour, grateful for the opportunity to rest our aching backsides at last, and soon a rope corral was erected and guards posted to watch throughout the night.

Small fires were lit and rations brought out. We hadn't eaten since that morning, and now we were ravenous, though the fare, some suspect bacon and soda crackers, could have been better. Slowly dusk descended upon us and eventually a fine drizzle began to fall, pattering against the exposed grass and dripping steadily from the boughs of the trees. The men erected crude wickiups made from branches, blankets and ponchos beneath which to shelter.

The evening passed slowly, and largely in silence. I could sense the edgy nervousness of the other men, and felt pretty much the same way myself. Then, around nine o'clock, Jack rose to his feet, checked his guns and then began to prepare his horse for riding.

'Where are you going?' I asked.

He glanced over one shoulder at me. 'To locate the Indians, of course.' Again, he made it sound so casual, as if he were really planning only to visit some neighbours whose company he greatly enjoyed.

His announcement sent a low murmur through the enlisted men. Gregson, sitting on a deadfall some feet away, stood up and came over. 'Is it wise to go on your own?' he asked.

A cynical smile twitched at the corner of Jack's mouth and a wicked gleam entered his gaze. 'Do you mean that there is actually someone here willing to go with me?' he countered.

The night was silent but for the dripping of rainwater, the low crackle of the cook-fires and the occasional, intrusive flapping of night-birds roosting high above.

'I'll go with you,' I said before I was properly aware that I had spoken.

He looked at me, and I was gratified to see that he was in no way surprised that I, out of all of them, should be the only one to volunteer. During the course of the day I had grown increasingly anxious to prove myself in some way, and conquer the fear that was gnawing at my vitals before it took too great a hold, and I was curiously disappointed when he shook his head. 'I appreciate the offer, Ash,' he said. 'But it's best I go alone. Less chance of being discovered.'

He toed in and swung across leather, and turned his black horse out into the darkness. After he was gone, Gregson came over to me and said, 'You know him pretty well, Colter. Is even *half* of what they say about him true?'

'At *least* half,' I replied.

He was gone for hours. I tried to stay awake until he returned, but it had been a long, arduous day and despite my fear, I could not fight my exhaustion. When next I opened my eyes, however, I saw by the glow of the shifting embers that Jack was back, just dismounting and crossing over to Lieutenant Gregson. Hurriedly I sat up and threw off my blanket, and knuckling sleep from my eyes, went over to join them. Jack looked at me and nodded a terse greeting.

'What did you find?' the lieutenant asked eagerly.

'There's a shallow draw about a dozen miles northeast of here. An unusual geographical feature for this part of the country. Anyway, that's where your Cheyennes have been hiding themselves. There's a rough kind of cavvy at one end, filled with stolen horses. The rest of the gully is taken up with tipis.'

'And their strength?'

'It was difficult to estimate with any accuracy. As you might imagine, the light was poor. But I should say there are perhaps fifty of them.'

'*Fifty!*'

'About thirty warriors,' Jack amended, much to our relief. 'The rest are women and children.'

Gregson digested that. 'Women and children,' he repeated thoughtfully. 'That puts a rather different complexion on the matter, doesn't it?'

'It does,' Jack confirmed. '*If* we take the fight to the Cheyennes. We'd have the element of surprise, true, for that is the last thing they'd expect us to do. But we'd also run the risk of injuring their dependents.'

'I've no time for Indians,' Gregson muttered. 'But neither do I wage war on the defenceless.'

'I'm glad to hear you say that, lieutenant,' Jack replied. 'Still, it leaves us with a pretty problem, and I do not deem it wise just to sit around and wait for the Cheyennes to attack us *here*.'

'Why not?' Gregson asked. 'We have the advantage of high ground.'

'But the Indians have superior numbers and greater experience,' Jack pointed out. 'No. If we're to win this little skirmish, we need to fight it on our own terms.' He rose from his crouch. 'Get your men up and ready to move, Gregson. We're leaving here.'

'You're not suggesting a retreat, I hope?'

Jack fixed him with a stern eye. 'I have never retreated from the enemy in my entire life, lieutenant,' he said in a cold tone. 'Neither do I plan to start now.'

'Then what—'

'Tell your men to leave these wickiups of theirs exactly where they are, and bank the fires nice and high. I'll explain the rest of it as we go.'

The men were awake by this time anyway,

and within moments we were all cutting our horses from the makeshift corral and saddling up. I put the time at somewhere around midnight. A fresh drizzle began to tip-tap against leaves and long grass. Fifteen minutes after the order had been given, we were ready to move off.

Jack led us out of the scrubby oak and down onto the rolling flats below. The gibbous moon lit our path with a silver-white shimmer. Our descent was slow and cautious, though we increased our speed a little when the ground levelled out beneath us. I chanced a look back over my shoulder at the bivouac we had just vacated. There was not much to see, save the amber flicker of the cook-fires reflecting dimly off the trees and scrub – just enough to give the impression that we were all still up there.

Jack took us away to the south, back the way we had come, but we were not in for a very long ride, a quarter of a mile, if that. Then we reined in and Jack began to give orders. He set two men to rig up a rope corral for the horses. Then he led the rest of us back towards the slope on foot, finally deploying us in small groups here and there about fifty yards out from the base of the slope, so that we were completely hidden in the long grass.

He gave strict instructions that we must maintain absolute quiet and act only upon his signal. He said that we were going to allow the Cheyennes to come right in and, as they thought, attack us while we slept. But if we were to make his plan work, we must do nothing to alert them before they were irrevocably in our sights, and he made it clear in no uncertain terms that he would deal harshly, and personally, with any man there who disobeyed his orders.

With the horses tethered safely out of sight and the men positioned to Jack's satisfaction, we finally settled down to wait. I am not certain now exactly what I felt at that time, but I am almost sure it was a combination of fear, apprehension, excitement and a curious and exhilarating sensation of being completely alive for perhaps the first time in my life.

'Keep your eyes open, Ash,' Jack whispered, breaking my reverie. 'Wake me up the minute you spot them coming.'

I thought for a moment that he was joking. 'You're not going to *sleep?*' I asked, incredulous.

'Of course,' he replied with a smile. 'A man must be at his freshest if he is to acquit himself well in combat. And the Cheyennes will not be here until just before dawn.'

'How can you be so sure?' asked Gregson, a few feet further along the line.

'Think about it, lieutenant. When does a man's spirit reach its lowest ebb? When does he sleep the deepest? They'll be here just before dawn, mark my words. And don't forget – they'll be coming a-foot, as quiet as ghosts, so be extra vigilant if you value your lives.'

And so saying, he lay down on his side, tilted his sombrero over his face and soon his breathing grew calm and rhythmic.

The night wore along, not slowly, as you might have expected, but all too fast. My eyes grew glassy from constantly staring into the darkness. The drizzle stopped. I wondered what the other men were thinking. I doubted they had ever been in such a situation before. This would be their first real fight. I hoped they would acquit themselves well, for I began to understand in those cold, waiting hours, that my survival depended upon their performance every bit as much as theirs depended upon mine.

I watched the long damp grass far ahead of me shiver and rustle for a long time without realising that it heralded the arrival of the Indians. By that time I had grown so fatigued by the simple act of waiting and watching, that I actually found myself following the progress of the first of the Cheyennes to come up off their bellies and into a crouch without properly realising just what I was seeing.

Then the braves began to snake up the slope, muscular bodies daubed for war, black hair shining wetly, clad only in breechclouts and moccasins, with cut-down rifles and clubs and tammixes in hand.

An electric tingle washed through me and I reached over and shook Jack awake. He sat up and pushed back his hat. He needed no telling what I had seen. He followed my line of vision and saw the warriors crawling up through the tall grass and smiled. 'They will come quickly now,' he whispered. 'They will be anxious to count coup. And their haste will be their undoing.'

He slid his Sharps rifle slowly up along his side and checked the mechanism. Following his lead, I inspected my Yellow Boy and wiped a light coating of moisture from the brass frame. I was dry in the throat and my heart was thudding so hard that I felt a little sick. But I knew I could not let these other men down, Jack least of all, for though they might not realize it, we were all relying on each other, now.

Again Jack had called it correctly, though, for the first of the Cheyennes were swiftly joined by the others, and the long grass around the base of the slope was shaking and swaying to mark the passage of yet more.

I swallowed and licked my lips. I told myself that if I could just keep my nerve, I would be all right. In the next moment, my eyes widened. A brave with an ornate feathered warbonnet with flowing trails was just beginning to ascend the incline, lance in one hand, club in the other.

'Ah,' muttered Jack, at my side. 'Here is the fellow I've been waiting for.'

I glanced at him. 'Is he their chief?' I asked. The slope was alive with Cheyenne warriors now, all snaking up towards the faintest fire-glow illuminating its summit.

'He's the one,' he confirmed.

He worked the Sharps' under-lever and loaded a cartridge into the open breech. Then he closed the breech gently, thumbed back the hammer, brought the weapon up to his cheek and sighted along the octagonal barrel. I watched him take aim at the Cheyenne chief and wondered how he could so calmly kill a man from hiding. But then, he had won fame as a sharpshooter during the War. Perhaps he had learned to switch off his emotions at such times as this and simply get on with the job.

When he fired the Sharps, I flinched, for the weapon had the deafening crash of a cannon, and the most devastating killing power. The warrior in the fancy warbonnet was slammed flat against the ground. He didn't even have a chance to cry out. As he began to slide lifelessly back down the slope, the Cheyennes around him were thrown into confusion.

Suddenly, right the way along the line of men Jack had deployed, I caught the sudden flash and spit of muzzle-flare and the boom and crack of gunfire. Its effect upon the exposed Cheyennes was awesome. That first volley claimed six braves, and they went down dead or dying. As they began to slide and roll down the incline, the night trembled to the sound of their furious yapping. More of them came up out of the long grass to direct their fire at us, and after that it ceased to be a turkey shoot and instead became a full-scale war.

We had thinned them out in those first few moments, which had been our intention, and that was a comfort, but it was a small one. Now, watching them come charging at us through the first faint greyness of dawn, I was almost paralysed with fear. Gunfire erupted along the line to my right and left. Jack's Sharps boomed again, and a face-painted brave virtually back-somersaulted into the grass and lay still but for the odd, gruesome kicking of one leg.

That broke the spell holding me captive, and I fired the Yellow Boy, worked the lever and fired again. I heard a man scream, turned that way and saw one of the enlisted men go backwards with a feather-adorned lance protruding from his chest. Someone called my name. It was Jack. I turned around and cried out in surprise, for they were almost upon us and it was going to be hand-to-hand at any moment.

I fired my Winchester again. A Cheyenne twisted around and fell to the ground, clutching his belly, from which there issued a flood of crimson. Gregson tossed his empty carbine aside, drew his Colt with one hand and sabre with the other, and threw himself into the fray. Jack came up from his kneeling position, fired one more round, then turned his Sharps around so that he could use it as a club.

Mindful that I may with some confidence number among my readers those of a sensitive humour – and even members of the fairer sex – I will moderate my account of that vicious fight as best I can. And in any case, though I feel duty-bound to give as full an account as I may, I have to confess that my recollections of all but the specifics are vague, at best. A brave whose face had been transformed into a hideous deathmask by the application of red and yellow paint threw himself upon me and we crashed to the ground in a wild tangle, each of us struggling for supremacy. I lost my precious

Winchester in the fall, but in another respect I was lucky that dawn, for at sixteen summers, my opponent was probably one of the youngest braves there, and I had little problem in wrestling him down onto his back and attempting to throttle him.

Young though he was, however, there was also a demonic strength in him, and his nails raked my face and the backs of my hands as he attempted to dislodge me, and his dark eyes were alight with a sort of killing madness. He tore a knife from his belt and I saw it just before he could open me up with it, and threw myself backwards, out of reach. Before I knew where I was, he was on his feet and I was on my back, and I felt sure that he would kill me any second. I reached down for my revolver, and snatched it from its pouch. Just as he leapt at me I pulled the trigger and my bullet tore him backwards, away from me. He fell, screamed, squirmed and died.

I got my legs under me and came up into a crouch, shaking. I spotted someone racing towards me and almost shot him, but saw a flash of army blue at the last minute and stopped myself. The soldier ran past me and clubbed another Cheyenne to death with the stock of his carbine. The skull beneath the braided black hair made a splintery, cracking noise.

'To horse, men! We've got them on the run!'

Gregson's voice penetrated the fog that had taken possession of my brain, and I blinked a few times and shook my head. We had got them on the run? The fight was almost over? I felt a hand touch my shoulder and I whirled around, ready to use my handgun again without hesitation if it meant the difference between living and dying, but then I saw who it was and Jack, looking a little startled, took a pace backwards and said, 'Whoa there, Ash. It's me.'

I looked around, aware that the yelling and shooting had finally stopped. The slope was littered with bodies. It was a grotesque vista, quite the worst I had ever seen. I shook my head again and spat to clear my gummy mouth. 'Have they...' I found it hard to organise my thoughts. 'Are they…'

'We've broken their back, Ash,' Jack said grimly. 'No more than a handful of them have made a break for it, and we're going after them.'

I realised that Gregson and his men were charging past us, heading for the horses. I scooped up my rifle and fell in beside them. I wanted to ask Jack how I had done, but kept silent. I was still alive and, apart from some scratches, I was unhurt, so I figured I had done well enough. The light was growing stronger now, and I attempted to take a quick tally of the soldiers. There were five of them, apart from Gregson and Sergeant Rawlings. That meant we had lost three – lighter casualties by far than those we had inflicted upon our enemies.

We reached the horses, flung ourselves up into our hulls and, with a ram of the heels, sent the animals shooting off across the gradually brightening plains. The morning wind brushed across my face, cooling my fevered skin. In the distance we saw where the Cheyennes had tethered their own horses, and that made us go all the faster, for we had to finish this dirty business the best way we could, to break this last pocket of resistance and arrange to have the survivors punished or packed off to the reservation in northern Indian Territory – which, in retrospect, I can see was pretty much the same thing.

About eight or ten of the Indians had survived the fight back at the slope. Now some of them turned to face us with their cut-down rifles winking flame while the rest threw themselves up onto their ponies.

Gregson yelled, *'Charge!'*, and before I knew it, we were among them, and horse was colliding with horse in the rising dust, men were yelling, guns were blazing, and we were using our handguns to club and hammer as well as to shoot, dodging knife, lance and tammix, fighting to put down our enemies, fighting to *win:* as, above us, the sun rose higher in the eastern sky, as red as the blood now staining the open prairie…

SEVEN

Were you to believe everything you read in the history books, you'd think we took on the entire Cheyenne nation that day. But I have the figures to dispel that myth right here beside me.

That party of Cheyennes who came down from the Powder River country to terrorise our neighbourhood in the summer of 1867 actually numbered sixty one. Thirty three of them were males, sixteen were females and the rest were children. Of the thirty one warriors who took part in the fight that dawn, seventeen were killed, eight were wounded and six were taken prisoner in the final rout. Because the government did not wish to antagonise the Indians any more than it could help, the survivors were simply shipped off to the Cheyenne reserve between the

Cimarron and Arkansas rivers. Later I heard that the surviving braves were among those who went on the warpath with the Kiowa and Comanche the following year.

But that last donnybrook, where it was kill or be killed, hardened me to battle, and I never again felt the same degree of fear at having to lock horns with another man. And though I took no pleasure from surviving at some other poor soul's expense, I did learn to enjoy the respect with which I was accorded upon our return to the Snake River station.

Mr Traylor was just as proud of me as any real father could be of his son, and whenever a coach pulled in or a traveller passed by he would put an arm around my shoulders and say, 'Have you met my hired man, Ash Colter? Ash was one of the men who routed them Indians we had trouble with a while back.' And with a squeeze or a light punch on the arm he would add, 'He's a regular tiger, our Ash!', and I would stand there and enjoy all the attention.

The adulation of others became like a narcotic to me. The more I had, the more I craved. But there was one problem. Life in those parts was, by and large, quite sedentary, and opportunities for a fellow to prove his worth came few and far between. I had always enjoyed the quiet life, for I was still basically a shy man, but now there was something inside me that demanded more.

Then, at breakfast one morning, Jack delivered some stunning news. 'I'll be moving on at the end of the week, if that's all right, Mr Traylor.'

I could hardly believe my ears. Jack Page had become something of a fixture around the station, save for those long periods when he would go off riding alone. It had not occurred to me that there would ever come a time when he wished to move on, as he put it. Now, as I toyed with my food, I wondered what life around the station would be like once he was gone. I did not like the answer.

'Moving on, Jack?' Mr Traylor said with a frown. 'Aren't you happy with us here?'

'It's not a question of being happy,' he replied. 'I came out here to recover from my injuries. Well, I've done that, and more. But I've never been a one to stay in the same place too long. It's nothing personal. You're all fine people. It's just my way.'

'Well … we'll all be darn' sorry to see you go,' Mr Traylor said, conveniently overlooking the fact that he himself had been planning to ask Jack to leave a few months earlier. 'But good luck to you.'

Later, as we were forking hay to the horses, I said the only thing I could think of to say. 'I haven't paid you back for my pistol yet.'

He smiled. 'Take it as a gift, Ash.'

'I'd rather pay my debts,' I said sharply.

He frowned, puzzled by the tone. It hurt me to think that my association with this man who had become like a big brother to me was finally going to come to an end, and although I knew that he was perfectly at liberty to go where he wished, when he wished, I was still just immature enough to feel that he was being unreasonable, and

149

that I was being treated unfairly because of it.

'All right,' he said after a while. 'When I reach wherever it is I'm going, I'll send you my address. You can wire me the money.'

I nodded. 'Good enough.'

He stayed out of my way for much of the week that followed, and I couldn't really say that I blamed him. As the days went by, however, I came to see just how unreasonable my behaviour was, and when his last morning with us dawned, I determined to make our parting as cordial as I could.

When he came into the common room, I saw that he was dressed exactly the way he had been when he first arrived; black frock coat, boiled white shirt, string tie, silk vest, loud check trousers, flat townsman's shoes and, of course, the twin .44s tucked into the crimson sash at his waist.

We were all lined up to say our goodbyes to him. Mr Traylor was the first to shake him by the hand and wish him all the luck for whatever the future held for him. When he came to Hetty, he once again swept off his sombrero, bowed low and kissed her hand. 'I will miss the beauty of your smile, the shine of your eyes, the sweet contralto of your voice,' he told her gravely. 'But most of all, Miss Hetty, I will miss your excellent herb dumplings.'

Up until he said that, I swear she had been on the verge of tears. Instead she gave an unsteady little chuckle and said, 'Aw, get away with you, Jack Page!'

At last he came to me, and when he extended his right hand, he found mine ready to take it. 'All the best to you, Jack,' I said sincerely, and he seemed to appreciate it.

Clapping me on the arm, he said, 'Look after yourself, Ash. We've shared some scrapes, you and I, but no man ever had a better partner to back him up.'

'I've saddled your horse,' I said, to cover my embarrassment.

'Just can't wait to be rid of me, is that it?'

'Was it that obvious?'

He put his hat back on and regarded us

all. 'Well,' he began.

But we never got to find out what else he intended to say, for at just that moment we were drawn to the window by the sound of horse-hooves, coming in fast.

The solitary rider was approaching from the east at a mad dash, leaning forward over the wildly-whipping mane of the bay horse. Only a sudden flash of corn-coloured hair helped us identify the rider, and Hetty muttered, 'That's Kate Spickett.'

She was an infrequent visitor to our station. I don't believe she came by to see us or buy supplies any more than a handful of times in the entire two years I had been there.

'Looks like trouble, the way she's pushin' that horse,' commented Cy.

It certainly did, and just as she sawed at her reins to bring the bay to a stiff-legged halt in the yard, making Jack's tethered mount sidestep skittishly, we hustled out into the morning sunlight to greet her.

'Trouble, Katie?' Mr Traylor asked, going forward to take her reins and calm the wall-eyed horse.

She was about thirty five years of age, but due to the skilful application of rice powder and rouge, Kate looked much younger. Her worried hazel eyes regarded us all, and because she was still breathless from her wild ride, she could only nod. She was a handsome woman with a full figure beneath her boys' size pants and shirt. Her hair was a mass of yellow waves and curls, her lips a scarlet heart above her strong chin, but I noticed that there was a dark, puffy flush on one of her cheeks, just below the eye, that she had tried to disguise; a bruise.

'Here,' said Hetty. 'Light a moment, I'll get you some coffee.'

She came aground and said, 'Thank God I got here in time!'

'What is it?' asked Cy. 'What's the matter, Katie–?'

'Walt!' she replied, wide-eyed. 'He told me he's coming out here today to make trouble for you! He says he's going to fix the lot of you!'

Mr Traylor frowned. 'Fix the – maybe you better explain yourself Katie. You're talking crazy.'

'I don't think she will have time to explain,' Jack cut in quietly.

We all saw them then, Walt Devlin, his brother Hal and their sister's husband, Tom Farson, riding stirrup-to-stirrup at an easy gait, coming in from the south, and Mr Traylor, perhaps not comprehending the possible threat these men represented, came around the head of the hard-breathing bay and said, 'Walt! Am I glad to see you. Maybe you can–'

Walt drew his sidearm, a big single-action Colt's Dragoon, and triggered a shot that shattered the morning air. Dirt sprayed up not two feet from Mr Traylor's boot-tips and he stepped back hurriedly, fighting the pull of the frightened horse.

'Hey, now, Walt! Wait–'

Walt and his kin rode into the yard and fanned out, then reined in about twenty feet ahead of us but did not dismount. I noticed that Hal was swaying ever so slightly, and Tom's freckled, pinched little face was even ruddier than usual. They had been drinking, and from the looks of them, their jag had probably lasted half the night.

Walt's hazel eyes fixed upon Katie and I sensed rather than saw the shiver that ran through her. 'So,' he said. 'I mighta guessed you'd come out here to warn 'em.'

'For God's sake, Walt,' she implored. 'Be reasonable about this!'

'*Reasonable!*' And here his eyes suddenly flared, and a stream of foul language issued from a mouth still faintly scarred by the injury Jack had inflicted upon it some time before. 'Damn you, Katie! Damn you *all!*'

Mr Traylor tied Katie's bay to the rail beside Jack's animal. I watched his clumsy fingers tremble. I knew he was not a courageous man, but to his credit he tried to face up to Walt again. 'Now listen here, Walt,' he said. 'We don't want no trouble here, and neither do you. If you've got a grievance, light and spit it out, and we'll do our best to settle it the neighbourliest way we can, but–'

'We've come for our money, Horace,' Hal broke in, and there it was, as if to confirm my suspicions, the slightest slurring of one word into the next. 'We're way overdue for a payment on this here land. Your precious Overland comp'ny hasn't paid us a red cent in better'n eight months, an' we're purely sick o' waitin'!'

Mr Traylor's forehead grew ridged. I have already stated that Walt had sold this piece of land to the company a couple of years earlier. But that had nothing to do with us, and Mr Traylor confirmed it with his next statement. 'Boys… If the company owes you money, you'll have to take it up with them. We only run the pl–'

Walt fired his Dragoon again and Mr Traylor screamed as meat and blood punched out of his right bicep and straight through his rolled shirtsleeve. He grabbed at his arm and collapsed onto his knees, and Hetty screamed and ran to help him. Kate and Cy both started talking at the same time, scared, trying to reason with Walt, but when he thumbed back the hammer again, they shut up.

'God help me, but you've kept me waitin' for my money long enough, Horace,' he husked.

'It's got nothin' to do with us!' Cy told him in a strained voice. 'Fer Crissake, Walt, look what you've done to him! You out of your mind?'

'I want my *money.*'

'Then you'll have to take it up with Wells, Fargo! They run the Overland now!'

'To hell with that. I come for my money, Cy, an' if I don't get it real soon, you'll take the next bullet.'

'Put up that gun, Devlin.'

All eyes turned to Jack as he stepped forward and casually tucked back the folds of his frock coat to allow easier access to his pistols. 'You've got no quarrel with these folks. Your fight is with me, and we both know it.'

'I'll be comin' to you in a minute, stock

tender,' Walt replied in that low, gravelly voice of his. 'I got me a whole string o' scores to settle this mornin'.'

'And I see you've already started with Miss Spickett here,' Jack remarked with a disgusted shake of the head. 'My God, but you're a sorry excuse for a man, Devlin. Step down from that horse and see how far you get trying to hit someone who can fight back.'

'She had them lumps a-comin'!' Hal broke in defensively. Walt turned in the saddle and tried to get him to shut up but he just kept going. 'I mean, how'd *you* feel if you found out there wuz another man pokin' your woman?'

'*Hal!*'

Suddenly I understood the real motive behind this visit of theirs; understood exactly where Jack had been spending all those long hours when the rest of us believed him to be out riding.

'Step down, Devlin,' Jack said quietly. 'I will take you on all together, or one at a time. The choice is yours.' To the rest of us he said, 'Get along inside, if you will. This may be bloody.'

'Walt,' Kate said, with a crack in her voice. 'This is getting out of hand, now! Calm down, *please,* before someone gets hurt!'

'It's too late for that, Kate,' said Walt, ominously.

Cy went over and with Hetty's help, lifted Mr Traylor back onto his feet and dragged him inside. I stood rooted to the spot, unable to move. 'Ash,' Jack said without looking around. 'Be so good as to escort Miss Spickett inside, will you?'

I blinked. Kate. She was still out here. I went over and took her by the arm. She tried to resist me. She wanted to stay right where she was and perhaps try to avert the impending fight, but I tugged her some more and at last she came with me, reluctantly, into the common room.

Hetty and Cy had set Mr Traylor down on one of the bench seats and were trying to tear his shirtsleeve away in order to examine the wound. Mr Traylor had his eyes squeezed shut, and was alternatively moaning and sobbing. Not trusting myself to speak because my heart was pounding so madly, I pushed Kate in their direction, hoping that she would occupy herself giving them a hand.

I ran my fingers up through my hair. Three to one. They were dire odds, and I wasn't sure that even the great Jack Page could handle them all on his own. Without pausing to consider the consequences, I hurried straight to my room and took my gun and holster from the peg in the back of the door.

I hustled back through the common room, buckling the belt around my hips and praying that I would be in time to lend a hand. As soon as I stepped outside, however, I pulled up short and gave a mental curse, because Kate had also returned to the yard in order to make one last attempt to stop this showdown, and I feared that her continued presence might just provide the spark to set the powderkeg off.

She was still standing halfway between Jack and the Devlins, her little hands balled into fists at her sides, her shoulders slightly hunched and stiff with tension as she looked up at the three riders. 'Please, Walt!' she was saying. 'I'm sorry. I know I shouldn't have done the things I did. It was a mistake. But it's not worth dying for!'

Walt's scarred lips twisted into something that was meant to be a smile but looked more like an expression of pain. 'You shoulda thought of that afore you betrayed me in the first place, you bitch!' he replied.

'Tell us, Katie,' Tom Farson said through a cold grin. 'Was Page here the only feller shared your bed, or were there others?'

'Could be she's been with half the men in the county, Walt,' opined Hal.

'Please, Walt!' she said again. 'If you want me to beg, all right – I'm begging! Come on, let's just leave here, now, you and me. I'll make it up to you, Walt. I'll be good for you, I promise I will–'

'Kate,' he said with a sigh. 'There was a time when there weren't nothin' I wouldn't do for you. But now, when I think of you an' him, together, I get sick to my stomach.'

And he brought his Dragoon up and around and fired it once, and the bullet slammed right into Kate's body, between her breasts, and she gave a sort of sigh and grunt all in one, and went over backwards.

I watched her fall. It was as if I were seeing real life slowed down, as you do sometimes in your dreams. I saw her with perfect clarity, her face, pale, with the disguised bruise, her eyes, filled with an expression of surprise and horror, the blood at her mouth and on her body, the awful looseness of her limbs. I thought, *Oh my God, he's killed her. He's actually killed a woman.*

Someone yelled, *'Damn you!'*

It was me.

And then we were into it.

I tore my Adams revolver from leather and just started blasting away at Walt and his kin. Looking back on it, I went a little crazy, for I just could not believe that Walt had done the terrible thing he had. I saw Tom's horse rear up, stagger and lurch sideways. I had not meant to harm any of the animals, only the humans, the stinking, woman-killing humans.

Tom kicked free of the stirrups and threw himself sideways as the animal crashed to the ground, kicking and screaming. He went for his gun and I fired at him but missed. Then he came up onto his toes and spun around with his shirt tearing apart and I saw Jack, from the edge of my vision, emptying both .44s into him.

Walt gave up trying to control his mount and leapt from the saddle. He hit the ground in a cloud of dust, rolled, then scurried for the cover of a trough on the far side of the yard. At once I dodged sideways, to put the tethered horses between me and him. The poor beasts were pulling at the reins, trying to free themselves and get away from the roar of the sixguns. I thought for one moment that they would actually uproot the tie-rail in their desperation.

Jack went out ahead, heedless of danger, firing the left gun, then the right, trying to make every shot count. Hal clawed for his Starr and loosed off a couple of shots, then got his horse turned around, jammed in his spurs and tried to get out of there. But as far as I was concerned, he wasn't going anywhere. I came around the horses, still mad as hell, sighted on Hal and emptied my gun at him. One bullet hit his horse in the rump and sent her plunging down and forwards, so that she collapsed and went into a forward roll, throwing Hal out ahead of her and then coming down right on top of him and smashing him to death.

At last Jack thought to seek cover. He found it behind a pile of chopped logs away to the left. Behind the trough, Walt fired a couple of shots, but drew no response. Then it was time for us all to reload.

It was a difficult manoeuvre, for my fingers were shaking just as much as Mr Traylor's had, and the squealing sounds of the wounded horse were enough to rattle any man's nerves. I heard sounds from inside the common room; Hetty screaming, Cy, telling her to keep down. Then Walt began shooting again and I ducked as splinters tore from the log wall behind me.

I tried to return fire, but it was tricky, because the tethered horses were shifting around, making it difficult for me to aim properly, and Walt's horse was still running loose in the yard, unsure which way to turn, and I figured I had killed enough animals for one day.

Jack finished reloading and the yard came roaring back to life with the sound of gunfire. Bullets thudded into the side of the trough. The surface of the water exploded and sent up a silvery shower that went everywhere. A window shattered. There was more scream-ing. Then Walt came up from behind the trough and made a run for his horse, thick legs pumping, hat flying off in his haste, revealing his midnight-black hair, snowy at the temples.

Jack broke cover just as Walt reached the animal, grabbed at the saddlehorn and threw himself up into the hull. He jammed his spurs into the horse's already-scarred flanks and yelled some encouragement for the animal to get going, but even as the horse bunched its muscles and prepared to spring into motion, Jack got Walt square in his sights and fired both his revolvers, and Walt screamed curiously high and stood up in the stirrups. He discharged his own weapon wildly into the ground, fell sideways from the saddle with blood on his side, and hit the ground. He writhed there for a moment, howling, then sat up, blood spreading across his chest and down out of his mouth. He brought his gun up again but by then Jack was right over him, both guns aimed and blazing.

His bullets smacked Walt in the face and forehead and shoved him, twitching, back into the dirt. He had no face left to speak of, hardly any cranium. It was all just pulp, so much pulp.

Jack turned, crossed to the wounded horse and dispatched it without ceremony. Silence but for the faint, dying echoes of gunfire and the muffled commotion inside the common room were the only sounds. I looked around the yard, at Walt, Hal, Tom, Kate, the two dead horses, and my lip curled. I wondered when all the killing would finally end – or indeed, if *ever* it would end.

EIGHT

Much has been written about the Snake River Shootout, as it came to be known, and its aftermath has also been discussed at some length by students of Western history, so I will only summarise it here, for there is still much of our story left to tell.

Suffice it to say that when Jim Ballew tooled the eastbound stage into the yard a few hours later, he left with two extra passengers, Cy Pollack and Mr Traylor. Upon reaching Franklin, Cy got Mr Traylor to a doctor and then went to report the shootings to the town marshal, T G Haslett. Three days later, the county sheriff, Allan Doyle, rode out to the station and formally arrested Jack and me.

Before Justice of the Peace Levi Kennett, we explained as much of the affair as we considered necessary, but having no wish to besmirch Kate Spickett's reputation – or Jack's, come to that – we chose to omit the real reason for Walt's visit that day, and instead concentrate upon the outstanding debt he had come to recover.

Witnesses were called. Among them were Cy, Hetty and a slowly-recovering Mr Traylor. Under oath, a couple of Lazy D men grudgingly confessed that they had heard Walt boasting drunkenly the night before the killings. He had said, 'I'm going to fix them sorry sonofabitches out at the Snake River station.'

It was, then, a clear case of self-defence, but even if it had been otherwise, I think we would have been discharged, for the Devlins were not well-liked in the county – even less so once news of Kate's cold-blooded murder got around – and most folks were just glad to see the back of them.

Thus it was that we left the county courthouse as free, if infamous, men. But the matter did not end there. Folks came out to the station and lined up to shake us by the hand and ask shyly if they could touch the butts of our guns. The editor of the Franklin *Courier* paid Cy Pollack fifty dollars for an exclusive eye-witness account of the gunfight. Suddenly I had all the attention and respect I could ever want.

And yet I did not care to stay in that neck of the woods and be forever known as one of the participants in the Snake River Shootout. Men of such dubious distinction inevitably attract challengers, fledgling gunmen anxious to prove their own worth by burning down their peers, and I had no desire to await their arrival. This, I think, was why Jack always preferred to move on after a time. Apart from that, there was the very real danger that Angela Farson, Tom's widow and the Devlins' sister, might engineer some kind of retribution against us.

Suddenly I began to cherish the anonymity I had lost. The only way that I could see to regain it was to leave the area and start up my life someplace else. But I found the prospect of leaving the station frightening, because I had put down roots there following my somewhat nomadic childhood, and I did not especially care to begin my wanderings afresh.

Still, there seemed to be little else for it, and so, about a week later, I plucked up courage and finally gave voice to the suggestion that had been on my mind for some time. 'Jack,' I said. 'I know you were planning to shake the dust of this place from your heels before that run-in with Devlin. What ... what say we shake the dust together?'

He appeared mildly surprised by my proposition. 'You would leave this place, Ash?' he asked quietly.

'I would sooner go than stay, yes.'

He considered it. I had no idea if his

association with Kate Spickett had been a casual thing based more upon physical, as opposed to spiritual attraction, and certainly he was not a man who discussed his emotions freely, but I believe that her death affected him deeply, and that he felt he had at least in part been responsible for it. Finally he nodded. 'All right, Ash,' he said. 'We'll leave tomorrow.'

If I had entertained any notions that we might find some other peaceful part of the country in which to put down roots, however, I was soon to be disappointed, for I believe I covered more miles over the next few years than I had previously done in the whole of my life put together.

They were not idle times, though, and our travels broadened my education and understanding considerably. I learned much from my companion – how to read sign and track, how to live off the land, the most effective way to draw and use my sidearm; I even learned something of cards from him, though he was not exactly the best teacher I could have asked for, even if he personally believed himself to be a player of some skill.

Some of you may have heard of the noted Oglala Sioux chief Red Cloud. Red Cloud it was who negotiated the treaty that ended white encroachment upon hunting-grounds traditionally considered sacred by the Sioux. But there continued to be friction between white man and red, and after a somewhat unsuccessful spell as a professional gambler, Jack secured us employment with the Department of the Missouri as scouts, based at Camp Supply, in Indian Territory. It was here, in fact, that we first met that overblown popinjay, George Armstrong Custer.

In the November of 1868, we acted as guides for Custer's expedition to the Washita River, where there lay a Cheyenne encampment of some size. It had been decided that the only way to beat the Indians, who could be a most effective enemy when they chose to be, was to attack them when they were at their most vulnerable – namely, in the winter – and then herded them north and west, into Indian Territory. Thus, we led eight hundred men of Custer's 7th Cavalry through the most appalling blizzard until, four days out of Camp Supply, we came upon our destination.

Now we received some hint of Custer's reckless nature, for his plan of campaign was simply to dispense with any form of reconnaissance and split his command into four units, each with orders to attack the village from every point of the compass the following dawn.

I had no confidence in the man, and felt uneasy with his plan, for if there was one thing above all others that I had learned from Jack Page, it was to know your enemy, and the terrain upon which you were to fight him. I confided my misgivings to Jack, who felt much the same way, and I even tried to talk Custer into holding back until we could make a proper scout of the valley, but so headstrong was he that in his tent that bitter night he said, 'I do not need lectures on tactics, Mr Colter. *I* am in command here. It is my decision to make, and I have made it.'

'I appreciate that, colonel,' I replied. 'But I'm not even sure these Cheyennes aren't already on reservation land.'

'Nonsense, man! I would hardly have been ordered to drive them in if they had already come in of their own volition!'

'Still, it wouldn't hurt to make sure,' said I. 'I could ride to Fort Cobb and check with the company commander.'

'I don't see that there is anything to be gained by that.'

'But what possible difference could an extra day or so make, colonel?'

'We will go ahead with my plan as it stands, Mr Colter.'

I looked at him there in the unflattering glow of the Argant lamp on the little table that stood between us. He looked thin and pale, very blond and not a little cruel. 'Colonel,' I said, 'you are a glory-hound. A damned glory-hound.'

He stiffened. 'I think you forgot yourself, sir!'

But in the first year or so since I had left the Snake River, I had learned at last to speak up and be damned. 'Are you so hungry to build your precious reputation that you would risk the slaughter of innocents so casually?' I asked.

Custer's jaw muscles worked, and his icy blue eyes narrowed on me. 'I'll have no more of your damned insubordination, Colter,' he replied. 'You are dismissed!'

Well, that was fine by me. As you might have guessed, I had no stomach for Indian fighting. There were no simple rights and wrongs to it; rather, it was just so many different shades of grey, and I was better off out of it. Many years later, however, I read one of those yellow-jacket novels in which Jack himself claimed to have spoken out against Custer that night, while *I* remained silent. But no matter. I did state at the outset that, when the lie painted a more flattering portrait than the truth, Jack had no qualms about adopting the lie.

Anyway, Custer's men attacked the village

the following dawn, and he was lucky – but then, I always did say that the Devil looked after his own. His men killed better than a hundred Indians that dawn, of whom perhaps forty were warriors who constituted any real threat to him. He burned the village – more than seventy tipis – and ordered the slaughter of seven hundred horses, and he performed the whole sorry deed to the strains of his damnable 'Garry Owen'.

Yes, he was lucky – more lucky than he realised, for that village was just one of several spread throughout the valley, and he was fortunate indeed to get out of there in one piece once the fighting was over, before the survivors could summon reinforcements. Even so, his Major Elliott and nineteen enlisted men were ambushed and killed by a party of neighbouring Arapahos, and though Custer could have sent additional forces to save them, his main concern by that time was just to get back to Camp Supply, his victory – if that is the right word – secure.

Incidentally, the Cheyennes *were* on

reservation land, and had been promised safety by Fort Cobb.

Indian fighting was a dirty business, but I stayed at it simply because Jack stayed at it. In time I came to see a resemblance between him and Custer that went beyond the physical, for both were big, flamboyant men with long hair and flowing moustaches. Neither man really disliked the Indians. Indeed, both professed a great respect for their wild, outdoor ways. But likewise, each man saw Indian fighting as a means to enlarge upon his reputation, and Jack most certainly did that. He was always the first to volunteer for any hazardous mission, just as he had been during the War, and though my account now begins to take an increasingly harsh view of him, it is not my wish to denigrate his efforts during that period, for he did face very real dangers whilst scouting, running messages from one officer to another across open, hostile Indian country, and so on.

By this time, 1870, the frontier was opening up fast to accommodate an influx of settlers from the east, and a steady flow of Texas longhorns was coming up the Chisholm Trail, that magnificent artery pioneered by Joseph McCoy three years earlier. Rough and ready cow-towns had grown up along this and similar routes, and though they were raw, untamed places, a man could make his fortune in them; his fortune and, of course, his name.

That is why we curtailed our association with the army and rode north to Elton, Kansas, a wild and woolly place if ever there was one, and while I found employment as a clerk at the Express office, Jack again set about practising his dubious skills as a gambler.

But violence continued to dog our trail, and we never seemed able to outdistance it. Only later did I come to realise that Jack attracted it like a magnet, and that the only way I would ever be free of *it* was to be free of *him*.

I had long begun to notice a subtle shift in

my companion's personality. Where before he had been content to keep his own counsel, he now became as rowdy as the men with whom he started to keep company. Saloons became his favourite haunts. He took to smoking big cigars, which he would pass around freely when the mood was upon him. I hesitate to call him a drunk, for he never exactly displayed any reliance upon alcohol, and in fact had a remarkable tolerance for whiskey. He could drink as much as three- or four-fifths before it began to have any affect upon him. But he did begin to drink steadily, and occasionally grew belligerent when it finally took hold of him.

There lived in Elton at this time a fellow by the name of Frank Black, who was a gambler of some note. A certain rivalry existed between him and Jack, for in their own way, each man needed to feel that he was tophand. Frank was tall, slim and elegant in black broadcloth, with a dark, swarthy complexion and a rather evil set to his thin lips. It was said that he ran a couple of sporting girls down in the red light area known as the Devil's Half-Acre.

Anyway, Jack got into a game of cards with him one evening and Frank took him for practically everything he was worth. Not content with that, Frank humiliated him further by forcing him to sign a marker for the balance of the debt, being some forty dollars.

From that time on, each man walked softly around the other knowing that sooner or later they would clash again, and that next time they would be armed with weapons that were deadlier than mere cards.

Jack decided to hold back on paying off the debt. It was a stupid, childish response, but to his mind, the longer he defied Frank Black, the stronger it made him appear to his new-found cronies. There was also the matter of Mariane Kellogg, widely known to be Black's woman. Jack just had to humiliate Frank in turn by wooing her away from him, which, in the event, he did quite successfully.

Inevitably, this rivalry of theirs was going to lead to the worst kind of trouble, and so it did, one fine day in the August of that year. I was working at the Express office one morning when suddenly the door was flung open and a thin young man from the bank next door gasped, 'Colter! You better come quick! Your frien's got hisself involved in a shootin'-match!'

With a curse I came around the counter, grabbed for my jacket and without a word to my employer, followed him out into the street, where he raised one hand to indicate the public square in which I could already see some of the locals gathering expectantly.

I hurried up the street until finally I reached the square and shouldered through the crowd to get a better view of the pro-ceedings. There I hauled up sharp. The two combatants were standing about seventy five feet apart. Jack appeared quite calm and unconcerned, standing there in the sun, but Frank appeared stiffer, more keyed-up, crouching slightly, turned sideways-on, right arm bent at the elbow, hand flexed into a claw above the butt of his .45. He had had enough of Jack's behaviour and had decided to do something about it – and if all I had heard about his skill as a pistolman was true, he might just be the fellow to stop my companion's clock at last.

'Don't come any closer, Frank,' Jack called out.

'I don't need to, Page!' Frank called back. 'I'll shoot your damned eyes out from where I stand right now!'

And he drew his gun, twisted around and fired the thing, but missed, and Jack, as calm as you please, drew one of his Remingtons, brought it up, steadied it with his other hand and fired back.

His bullet caught Frank in the chest and threw him back into the dust. He went down with the looseness of death clear to see in the flapping of his arms, the way his head flopped about on his neck, the way his legs just fell out from beneath him.

A hush descended over the town. For a

moment I thought that the world had stopped turning, that every man, woman and child God had ever created had come here to witness this one brief explosion of violence.

Then one of the onlookers started clapping, and one by one the others joined in, and soon they were applauding him, actually applauding and cheering him for having killed a man to whom he had owed money and not paid, and whose girl he had deliberately set out to take away from him. It turned my stomach to see it.

After that little display, Jack began to get a bit too big for his britches, and one evening over supper, he confirmed my opinion when he announced, 'I'm going to run for county sheriff, Ash.'

I stared at him across the table. 'You? What do you know about keeping the peace?'

He ignored the disdain in my remark, or perhaps he was so fired up by his own renewed celebrity that he just didn't recognise it. 'I know enough to see that these are wild times we live in, and that any man who carries a star can make a name for himself.'

'You've already made a name for yourself,' I pointed out.

'Perhaps,' he allowed. 'But an ambitious man can always find a way to make the name bigger.'

So he ran for county sheriff and he won it in a landslide, and that was how I came to serve as his deputy. But the months that followed were marked by the same violence that had haunted us ever since he first came into my life more than three years earlier. Indeed, if anything, I believe the violence escalated.

You may, of course, ask why I stayed with him. It is a good enough question. And in truth, I am not sure. Perhaps he retained just enough of the old Jack Page to make me want to continue our association for as long as I could. Perhaps I entertained the hope that this was but a temporary phase he was going through, and that once we finally upped stakes and moved on again, his character would return to its old humour.

But then again, perhaps it was simply fear; fear of branching out and making my own way in the world. I was twenty three then. I should have been settled, with a regular job, a wife, children here and more on the way. But my nomadic life had made it impossible to call any place home. I had acquaintances, yes, but no real friends. He was the one stable element of my life, and I felt that it would truly set me adrift to finish my association with him.

I have said that Elton was a raw and untamed town, and thus Jack enforced the law in a raw and untamed manner. He took to carrying a Greener shotgun under his arm, and would use it without hesitation if he thought it would teach the lawless element to behave. In the face of such a stern opponent, most potential trouble-makers learned to toe the line, and we had no great problems with them. Sometimes, however, things got entirely out of hand.

The history books tell of one such

encounter, with a fellow called Sam Toplis, who was a teamster originally from Missouri. Toplis came into town one afternoon and spent what remained of the day raising Ned like there was no tomorrow. Although we didn't realise it at the time, he had been a border ruffian back in the '50s and, having recognised Jack on an earlier visit as a former Free State Militia man, had decided to engineer some sort of confrontation in which he could make Jack pay for what he perceived to be some longstanding injustices.

Anyway, there was Toplis, raising hell down at the Brink House, a combination saloon and hog ranch on the south side of town, and there was Jack and I, hurrying to deal with him, little realising that we were walking straight into a trap, and that the disorderly drunk we were expecting to deal with was in reality stone-cold sober, and with murder in his heart.

As soon as we entered the bar, things grew quiet. I stood just inside the batwings, my old Yellow Boy cradled in my arms, while

Jack strode right into the centre of the smoky room. The patrons eagerly cut a path for him. We saw their frightened faces. Jack asked them what all the disturbance was about, but no one answered him.

Then I caught a movement from the corner of my eye. Toplis had been lurking in the shadows to the right of the swing doors. Now he grunted something – I'm not sure what – and went for iron.

I yelled, *'Jack!'*

But Jack had seen and identified him the minute we entered the place, and anticipating such an act of perfidy, was already reaching for his own guns. He turned quickly, fell to a crouch and triggered two fast shots. One of them hit the wall just above the ornery teamster's head, the other caught him smack in the face and killed him outright.

I had never truly grown hardened to such sights, but I suppose to a certain extent I had come to accept them, for even then I had learned to link sudden, violent death with my companion. What turned my stomach more that day was the way in which this latest killing was greeted. The band struck up a lively jig in Jack's honour, and practically every man in the place queued up to slap him on the back and buy him a drink. It was this casual, callous acceptance of death that sickened me more than anything else, and in the weeks that followed I took to watching the onlookers at every fight in which Jack took part, always concentrating upon their eyes. They would glow with excitement at the prospect of impending death. Their feeble intellects could not grasp what a truly terrible thing it was to snuff out the life of another human being. To them it was only an act to be praised and pored over, an entertainment choreographed for their own personal gratification.

Fort Tremain lay but a few miles to the east of us, and a large percentage of our trouble came from off-duty soldiers. I remember one such incident especially well, for if I had not seen it with my own eyes, I would not have believed it possible for any man to have dared pull such an old trick and still get away with it.

Terry O'Hare was an enlisted man who came into town as often as possible and always ended up in trouble. He was a big, ruddy-faced Irishman with a vile temper, and on this particular occasion, he beat up the owner of Starke's Saloon and almost killed one of the percentage girls. When Jack and I went to arrest him, we found him in the centre of the street with his Colt already drawn, just waiting for us.

'Come ahead, *marshal*,' he slurred, and with a waggle of the gun, he added, 'Damned if I ain't got you beat this time, eh?'

Jack stepped down into the street and shrugged. 'I sure can't argue with that,' he replied. Then, looking at some non-existent deputies behind the Irishman, he said, 'Don't shoot him, boys. He's drunk.'

And O'Hare was indeed just drunk enough to fall for it. He turned around to face this new and unexpected threat, then realised –

too late – that he had been suckered. Before he could swing back to face Jack, Jack drew one of his guns and shot him dead.

One midnight about a week later, the door to the law office flew open and Jack marched in a staggering, blue-clad army officer. The man was tall and angular, thin-faced, with a flushed complexion, centre-parted brown hair and a small, tufted beard at his chin. He was saying, 'I'll see you in hell for this, Page! So he'p me, I'll see you in hell!'

Jack only laughed. 'You're drunk, Custer,' he said. 'You'll feel differently in the morning.' He turned his attention to me. 'Lock him up for me, will you, Ash?'

I came out from behind my desk and turned up the guttering lamp, the better to see the prisoner. 'That's not Custer,' I said, disappointed that I would not have the pleasure of locking up the so-called, 'Boy General'.

'It's his brother, Tom,' Jack replied. 'I found him drunk as a lord, staggering down the centre of Main and trying to shoot out the municipal lights.'

Swaying, Custer said, 'You have no right to arrest me, damn you!'

'Shut up,' I said. 'And get into that cell.'

He focused on me with a mighty effort. His eyes were blurry and glazed. 'Hell, that's rich, a kid giving *me* orders! Do you know who I am, kid? See these baubles on my tunic here? Medals of Honour, boy, Medals of Honour! An' I won two of the bastards! *Two!* Is this how you treat a hero?'

'Just get into that cell, Custer,' Jack said, coming over to give him a shove. 'And boast about those medals when you're fit and sober enough to do them justice.'

We wrestled him into the cell and held him there until ten o'clock the following morning, and when at last he climbed aboard his horse – which someone had found tethered outside Starke's place – and set out on the long journey back to Fort Tremain, he quickly became the object of considerable ridicule. He was crumpled and sick-looking, hardly able to stay in the saddle. Not even his precious Medals of Honour could help him restore his lost dignity that day.

But the Custer arrest was to have sinister repercussions. Two days later, we heard that a fight had broken out between five drunken soldiers down at Starke's. 'I'll go,' Jack said tiredly, reaching for his shotgun.

'Can you handle it alone?' I asked.

'Of course,' he replied with his customary confidence. 'There are only five of them.'

I stood in the doorway and watched him stride away. It was the middle of a bright, autumnal afternoon, and winter was already feeling crisp in the air. I had a bad feeling as I watched him go. I should have gone with him. I should have, but I didn't.

Jack reached the saloon and pushed inside. 'All right!' he snapped. 'Break it up, here!'

But no sooner had the words left his lips than the five brawling troopers turned upon him and, after a brief scuffle, during which the shotgun was torn from his grasp and kicked out of reach, he was dragged to the sawdusted floor.

To hear Starke tell it afterwards, they went at him like a pack of rabid wolves, punching, kicking, stomping, until he curled into a ball with no other course of action open to him but to take the punishment as best he could, and bide his time until the moment came when he could fight back.

Starke yelled at them to stop it, that he had had enough, but once a man's blood is up, there is no place for reason in his thinking, and so they just continued to kick and hammer away at him.

It probably did not last that long, but by the same token, it probably lasted a lifetime. Eventually the soldiers began to tire, and the blows grew less frequent and forceful, until at length they all just stood over him, flush-faced, hard-breathing, almighty proud of themselves.

It was then that Jack rolled over, taking them all by surprise, and started to use the .44 he had managed to free from his sash with his left hand. He discharged the weapon swiftly into the nearest target and the bullet struck one of the troopers in the throat and flung him backwards with a liquefied gurgle.

At once panic broke out among the bully-boys. As they scattered, Jack forced himself up onto his knees and fired the handgun again. The shell caught one of the fleeing soldiers in the small of the back and shoved him out through the batwings and into the street, where he died almost before he struck the boardwalk.

Inside the saloon, everyone was yelling at once. Biting on the pain racing through his bruised body, Jack tossed his Remington aside and flung himself toward the shotgun. Snatching it up, he swung it around on the first quick flash of army blue that came into his vision. Two of the troopers were racing up the stairs to his left. Presumably the whores' cribs were the handiest places in which to seek refuge. Jack discharged the Greener at them, both barrels, and the effect was awesome. Baluster rails shattered and the fleeing soldiers abruptly slammed face-first into the wall, then toppled sideways and tumbled back down to the ground floor, their flesh pulped by buckshot.

Tossing aside the smoking shotgun, Jack used numb fingers to tear his right-side Remington from his sash. He brought it up to line on the fifth trooper, a youngish, pock-faced fellow by the name of Haskins, and thumbed back the hammer. His face was bruised and cut. Blood stained his nostrils and lost itself in his moustache. It dribbled from his split lips to spatter his boiled white shirt.

Haskins' eyes opened wide and he held both hands up, palms out. 'No!' he yelped. 'For mercy's sake, Page, don't shoot! I was against it from the start, I swear! It was Custer put us up to it!'

Jack looked at him along the barrel of the gun. Custer. Evidently a bad enemy to have made. He spat a mixture of blood and saliva off to one side, then turned his attention back to Haskins, who was framed there in the still-swinging doors, half-crouched, hands still raised palms forward, as if for protection.

'Please, Page!' he cried. 'Let me go! I swear to God I'll never set foot in town again!'

Maybe he meant it and maybe he didn't. We will never know for sure, because Jack tightened his finger on the trigger and the handgun belched flame and thunder, and Haskins jerked sideways to smash against the wall, belly-shot. He slid down the wall and died kicking thirty minutes later.

NINE

It was inevitable, I suppose, that sooner or later Jack's violent ways would make things too hot for us in Elton. Suddenly his enemies included not only Tom Custer, but practically every enlisted man who rode into town, for he had accounted for so many of their number that they began to wonder if he didn't have some personal grudge against them. While recovering from the beating he had taken – a beating, I might add, that left him with an assortment of minor, though troublesome, injuries, including several cracked ribs – we heard a rumour that Custer had lodged a formal complaint about his behaviour with none other than Lieutenant General Philip Sheridan himself.

The time had come for us to move on yet again, and this we did during the spring thaw of '71, when we took to riding for the US Marshal's office in Denver, Colorado. Here, Jack built up a most creditable number of arrests, including the apprehension of numerous deserters and rustlers of government beef, while my particular gift of letters and ciphers kept me occupied in a more clerical and administrative position.

It was an eventful period for us, but since several books have already been published covering that part of our lives – and I have four different ones right here on the shelf next to the fireplace – I do not propose to go over the same ground yet again. Rather, I will move our story along by some four years, specifically to the fine summer's afternoon that a note arrived at our board-ing-house from a fellow by the name of Walter Murphy, asking us if we would dine with him at his hotel that very evening.

Intrigued by this invitation, for we had no idea who Murphy was, we sent a note back saying that we would be delighted, and sug-gested a time we trusted to be mutually con-venient. After all, we had nothing to lose.

Walter Murphy turned out to be a dapper little gentleman of direct manner and agree-able humour. He was a short, portly man of some fifty years, with a pale, jowly face, easy grey eyes and a personable smile. He arrived right on time in the hotel's opulent lobby, where we introduced ourselves and shook hands, and then he led us into the adjoining restaurant, where we took a corner table and ordered food while a string quartet played discreetly in the background.

Murphy, it transpired, was a businessman who had come out from the east many years earlier and made a name for himself as something of an entrepreneur. He dabbled in anything that he judged could turn a profit, no matter who outlandishly or seemingly impossible, and invariably made money – lots of money.

'And how goes life for you good gentlemen?' Murphy enquired affably. 'I must say, Mr Page, that I have followed your exploits for several years now. Yours too, of course, Mr Colter.'

I nodded graciously.

'I suppose you are wondering why I invited you here tonight?' he asked.

'The thought had crossed our minds,' Jack admitted, reaching for the whiskey decanter in the centre of the table and pouring himself a healthy slug.

'I'll come straight to the point, since we are all busy men,' Murphy said. He fixed Jack with a penetrating look and said, 'Have you ever heard of a place called Yellow Creek, Mr Page?'

'Of course,' he responded. 'It's a gold-town in Dakota Territory, isn't it? Just the other side of the Black Hills?'

Murphy beamed. 'I cannot fault your geography, sir. Cigar?'

I declined but Jack said, 'Thanks.'

As Murphy passed one across and then struck a match, he said, 'I represent the people of Yellow Creek, Mr Page. I have taken an interest in their affairs, and I suppose I am the nearest thing they've got to a city major.

'Well, if you've heard of Yellow Creek, you've doubtless also heard about its ... reputation. It is a lawless town, gentlemen. With gold currently fetching upwards of twenty dollars an ounce, you can imagine that it's dog eat dog up there. We need someone to come in and tame it, and we were hoping that you might consider taking up the challenge.'

Jack did not reply at once. He drew on his

cigar, blew smoke into the air, then inspected the tip of his stogie thoughtfully. A waiter arrived and set out our starters, something with fruit and jelly and a rich, whiskey-tasting sauce.

'Why don't you ask the government to send you a marshal, Mr Murphy?' Jack asked at length.

Murphy leaned forward over the table in order to speak conspiratorially. 'The government doesn't recognise our town, Mr Page. By some unhappy chance, it has grown up on reservation land previously granted to the Sioux.'

'Then you have problems with the Indians as well?'

'Occasionally, though not as much as you might think. I'll be honest with you. Yellow Creek is an inaccessible place. It can only be reached through a long, narrow pass that is easily defended, so Indian attack is not one of our gravest problems.'

'What is the population of your city, Mr Murphy?'

'Difficult to say. Three thousand. Maybe three and a half.'

'And the salary you're offering…?'

'We thought one hundred and fifty dollars a month.'

I paused with my spoon halfway to my mouth. One hundred and fifty dollars a month! It was an unheard of sum. But when I looked across at Jack, he was regarding the tip of his cigar again, profoundly unimpressed. 'Yellow Creek must need law and order quite badly for you to offer such a sum,' he commented, finally looking Murphy in the face again. 'However, my companion and I could not possibly undertake such an assignment for less than two hundred and fifty dollars a month, each – plus fifty percent of all the fines we collect.'

'*Each?*' Murphy gasped. 'That is impossible, sir! And in any case, we have only budgeted for one man alone, the city marshal.'

'Then I am afraid we have nothing further to discuss,' Jack replied cordially. 'In the first place, if Yellow Creek is as wild as you say it is – and I see no reason to doubt you – then it will most certainly be a two-man job to tame it. And in the second place, where *I* go, my partner goes.'

In an earlier time I would have filled with pride to hear him say such a thing, but now, listening to him, I felt that I was considered more as a kind of good-luck talisman than a man, a faceless thing not used to thinking or feeling or acting for itself. It also irked me that he had taken it upon himself to bargain for the two of us, with no prior consultation with me. No – he had grown too used to me simply going along with whatever he said, and this business was no different. And yet, when I think back on it, I realise it was in fact *very* different.

'I cannot meet your terms, Mr Page,' Murphy said at last.

'Then I am sorry if you feel you have wasted your time.'

Murphy looked at us. 'You will not consider the job for less than … two hundred and fifty dollars?' he asked hopefully.

'Plus the percentage I quoted,' Jack reminded him. 'No, Mr Murphy, I fear not.'

The dapper businessman sighed. 'Very well, then, Mr Page, Mr Colter. I agree to your terms, albeit reluctantly. If we may shake on it now, I will have contracts of employment drawn up for your signature in the morning. How soon can you start?'

'We'll be in Yellow Creek within the fortnight,' Jack promised, again without consulting me.

Later that night, as I climbed into my bed and lay staring up at the darkened ceiling, I thought about this new development. I did not especially want to leave my job with the US Marshal's office. It was interesting, reasonably well-paid and secure. I had put down roots in Denver, though I had not sunk them as deep as I would have liked, knowing that inevitably the time would come when Jack decided that we should move on.

But now I had a choice. I could tell him that I had come far enough in our wanderings, and that I would go no further. I could shake him by the hand and wish him all the luck and then watch him head north and probably never hear from him again. But we went back a long way together. Eight years. I had no one else, only him. And so I knew I would go with him, uncomplaining, and in a way I hated myself for it. Still, I felt sure that the time was coming when I must cease to be this faceless mascot of his, and become instead a man in my own right. Our relationship must progress beyond that of teacher and pupil. We were equals now, though evidently Jack did not see it that way.

We signed Murphy's contracts of employment and tendered our resignations with the marshal's office, and a week later we embarked upon the long journey up through Colorado, across the Great Plains of Nebraska and on into Dakota Territory, a journey of a little under four hundred miles. Some of it we covered by rail, but because the railroad did not extend that far in those days, we covered most of it by horse.

Much has been written about Yellow Creek, and I must confess that nearly all of it is true. It really was the wildest of towns, far wilder than Elton. As we neared our destination, we rode warily, for we knew that the Sioux would not be taking very kindly to the presence of so many white men trespassing on their sacred lands. But we saw no one, for it was a land of great immensity, all sheer rock walls and bubbling streams and steep, heavily timbered hills.

Eventually we saw signs of habitation. A rutted, winding track found its way under our horses' hooves. We passed a few high-sided wagons being driven by big, brawny men. Some of them were heavily guarded by hardcase-types toting rifles or shotguns, I looked into their eyes as we rode by. They were hard, cruel, suspicious: killers' eyes for sure. The kind of eyes my companion had developed over the years.

At length we came upon the narrow pass Murphy had spoken of. It was barely wide enough to allow two wagons to pass each other. We rode deep into the gorge. It was a claustrophobic experience, for the seamed rock walls were so steep that the sky existed only as the thinnest of thin blue bands high above us. We rode through cool grey shadow, passing miners on horseback or in heavy wagons every once in a while.

The pass opened out about a mile down the trail and we reined in on a muddy ridge to get our first look at Yellow Creek.

There was almost too much to see all in one go. The town had grown up along the floor of a fairly constricting valley, so there was only room for one long, winding street. The buildings lining it were nearly all single-storey structures, although there were a few that rose higher. Almost without exception they were of clapboard construction, already much-weathered, and each one was of a different dimension to its neighbours.

An endless procession of shingles proclaimed the services of liquor dealers, dentists, printers, attorneys, druggists and various other stores. There were several sporting houses and saloons, and even a couple of theatres. As you might have guessed, there were no churches.

Cut lumber was piled everywhere. The crowded boardwalks seemed to slide right down into the rutted, muddy street. Everywhere I looked I saw signs of activity. Rough-looking miners or speculators loitered here and there along both sides of the street. Wagon traffic was the heaviest I think I've ever seen. Buckboards and the odd, out-of-place surrey slid through the churned-up mire alongside bigger, uglier freight wagons. Pedestrians dodged between vehicles and riders alike to cross from one hectic boardwalk to the other.

And away behind each side of the street, emerald green, wooded hills rose in a steep climb, dotted with placer miners and their rough shanties, tents or dug-outs.

I sensed Jack's eyes on me and turned my head. He was smiling. 'Looks like a nice, quiet little town, don't you think?' he asked.

I smiled back. 'My biggest concern,' I replied dryly, 'is that we might die of boredom.'

We laughed for there was, of course, fat chance of that. Then we sent our animals down the trail and into town, where Walter Murphy had quarters at the only hotel in Yellow Creek, the grandly-named Sultan's Palace.

Although I do not intend to bore you with every small detail of our stay in town, I do feel there are a few things worth mentioning.

The most immediate of these was our accommodation, for there wasn't any. The townsfolk had not yet seen fit to build a jailhouse, so we were given a tent on an empty lot mid-way down the street; a tent, and a promise that a law office would be erected for us within six months.

Well, there was nothing to be gained by complaining about it, so we made the tent as comfortable as we could, and were just grateful that it was summer, otherwise we would have frozen to death within its draughty confines.

News of our arrival circulated quickly, and we rapidly became the object of much scrutiny. Most of the townspeople had heard of Jack, of course, and now they began to wonder what changes he intended to make in order to clean up their lawless town.

Wisely, Jack chose to do very little at first. Instead he would patrol the town ceaselessly, shotgun underneath his arm, just getting to know the feel of the place and the nature of its problems. These patrols were also invaluable when it came to identifying the men – and sometimes women – upon whom we should keep a special eye.

We were fortunate in that most of the trouble-spots were confined to the area at the farthest end of town known locally as the Badlands District, and it was here that we soon decided to concentrate most of our efforts. It was an awful hell-hole up there, where disease-riddled sporting girls turned tricks for fifty cents a time and many a drunken miner lost his life – and his claim – to the swift glint of moonlight on knife-blade.

In those few weeks we closed down six saloons for various reasons, mostly to do with murder, attempted murder, running crooked games of chance or serving up watered drinks. One of them was so notorious that Jack not only closed the place down and fined the owner, Sid Jessup, heavily, he also put a torch to the place and razed it to the ground.

But the enforcement of law sometimes had its lighter moments as well. One evening we were called out to one of the sporting houses, where a percentage girl was slashed across the face by a fat-bellied, liquored-up miner named Keegan. As soon as we burst into the place we saw from the look of him that Keegan would be more than happy to make a full-blown fight out of it. But all Jack did was bring his shotgun up and say, 'Drop that knife, Keegan. You haven't killed the girl, so it's only going to be a fine this time.'

211

Keegan threw back his head and laughed. 'A fine, is it? An' what am I supposed to pay it with? I'm flat-broke.'

Jack didn't bat an eyelid. 'If you can't pay the fine,' he said, 'you go to jail for forty eight hours.'

Again Keegan's face split with a grin that revealed his yellow, gappy teeth. 'Go to jail?' he repeated, obviously tickled by the notion. 'Hell, how you plan to throw me in jail, marshal? You ain't *got* no jail!'

Jack's moustache lifted slightly with a smile of his own. 'Toss down that knife and I'll show you how I'm going to do it.'

Curious, Keegan decided to be a good sport about it. He threw the knife to the floor, spread his hands and said, 'All right. Jail me.'

'Fair enough. You know where my tent is. Let's get down there.'

The miner did as he was told and we followed after him, keeping him covered all the while, for he could be an unpredictable cuss, could Keegan. As we made our way back down the street, I realised that most of the other patrons were following us, intent on seeing just how Jack was planning to make good on his promise. The night was dark but warm, the street illuminated by guttering torches hung in brackets at regular intervals along the boardwalk.

At length we came to the empty lot in the centre of which sat our lowly tent. The miner came to a halt and turned to face us. 'All right, Marshal,' he said. 'I'm waitin'.'

We all were, myself included.

Jack indicated the open space behind the tent. 'Go over there,' he said. 'And lay down.'

'Whut?'

'You heard me. Ash – fetch me a tarpaulin from one of the stores, will you? Tell them to charge it to the city council.'

I fetched the tarpaulin and watched as Jack opened it out, threw it across the prostrate miner and then weighted it around the edges with some hefty rocks. Next he drew one of the onlookers from the crowd, a short, skinny man wearing a cap, whose name was Isaacs. 'You wear a gun,' he said. 'Do you know how to use it?'

'A 'course I know!' Isaacs replied testily.

'Then you just became a deputy, Isaacs.'

'Eh?'

To the huddled form beneath the tarp, Jack said, 'Can you hear me, Keegan? You're staying under this tarpaulin for forty eight hours. If you try to get out from under there before time, Deputy Isaacs here will shoot you. Do you understand me?'

A muffled voice beneath the tarp said, 'Are you serious, marshal?'

'I'm *deadly* serious,' Jack replied. 'Because if Deputy Isaacs here lets you get away, then *I'm* going to shoot *him*.'

It was a neat enough trick, and it won Jack a lot of admirers, because after the audience got through laughing, they started to applaud him, and this time I found myself clapping right alongside them.

There was the danger that you could clamp down too hard on what went on in the

Badlands District, however, and if you did that, you became unpopular with everyone. So, though we did our best to clean up the dirtiest operations there, we gave the rest a loose rein to get along with and they seemed to respond to that. I would not exactly say that we reformed the low-lives who were drawn to the place to buy and sell liquor and sex, but certainly they learned to toe the line and seldom overstep it, and as a result the number of fatalities dropped within a month of our arrival, as did the general level of complaints to the city council.

As foul as it was, however, the district held a fascination for Jack that I could never understand. Sometimes it seemed that he spent his every waking moment down there, playing cards at a watering-hole called the Prospector's Rest, while I got on with the business of keeping the peace. He became great friends with the owner of the place, an oily, scheming fellow by the name of Bob Shambaugh, and that surprised me, because Shambaugh was well-known around town as a conniver, a conscienceless crook with a finger in every dirty business that could make money. I had even heard that he supplied young boys and girls to some of the miners who preferred to entertain such deviations, and I had promised myself that if I ever got proof to back that up, I would run him out of town on a rail. I could not see what he and Jack could possibly have in common, but then, they do say that opposites attract.

Neither had Jack's skill at cards improved over the years, and yet he continued to play, sometimes all day long. I heard that he lost more often than he won, and frequently quite heavily, and I did not see how he could possibly afford to pay off all his markers, even on the generous salary we were being paid. The mystery deepened when he revealed one evening that he had purchased a half-share in the Prospector's Rest.

'That must have cost a pretty penny,' I remarked, keeping my tone neutral. 'Have you taken up the bank-robbing business and forgotten to tell me, Jack?'

He ignored the question behind the question. 'It's a shrewd investment,' he said as we ate our evening meal by the smoky, low amber light of a flickering lantern. 'It's in places like the Prospector's Rest that the real gold is to be found, not up there in the hills.' Then he seemed to remember something, and setting his plate aside, he reached into his frock coat. 'I almost forgot,' he muttered. 'This is for you.'

And he offered me a thick stack of twenty-dollar bills.

I looked at them, but made no move to reach out and take them. There was something about them that jangled warning bells in my head. 'What's that for?' I asked cautiously.

'Bob Shambaugh asked me to pass it along,' he replied. 'It's two hundred dollars.'

'I can see that,' I said. 'I asked what it was *for.*'

He smiled. 'Shambaugh thinks we're doing a good job down in the District. He wanted to show his appreciation.'

'I take my pay from the city,' I said.

'What's that supposed to mean?'

I did not want a confrontation with him, so I just said, 'Nothing. Just that I don't want Shambaugh's money. If I took it, he might think that I owed him something.'

Jack was silent a long time before he said, 'This isn't a bribe, Ash. Shambaugh's a businessman. He likes to keep his relationship with the law as cordial as he can.'

I reached out to flip the edge of the stack in his hand. 'And that's the way he does it?' I asked. 'You know as well as I do that Bob Shambaugh waters his whiskey, rigs his games and sends half his customers away with the pox, Jack. But because he pretends to be such a generous fellow, you turn a blind eye to all that. Well, that's up to you. But I'd as soon treat everyone the same, and be beholden to none of them.'

Slowly he put the money back into his pocket. 'That's a little high-minded, isn't it?' he asked mildly.

'It's just the way I am,' I replied. 'No favours. One law for all.'

He brought out one of his fat cigars and struck a lucifer on his thumbnail. 'Shambaugh's offered us the finest suite at the Prospector's Rest,' he said. 'But I take it you'd sooner stay out here, in case it compromises you.'

I ignored the taunt in his voice. 'That's about right,' I told him. 'And if you had any sense, you'd steer clear of Shambaugh yourself. Christ almighty, Jack, how do you think it looks to the rest of the town, the way you've been carrying on?'

'Have a care, Ash,' he warned ominously. 'I've killed men for showing me less disrespect.'

'I know,' I shot back. 'I've spent the last eight years counting the bodies.'

We looked hard at each other. The positioning of the lamp threw shadows up across our faces, making us each look like a ghost, and it struck me in that moment of confrontation that in a way we *were* ghosts;

ghosts of the less complicated, better men we had once been.

'Look at you,' Jack said, shaking his head. 'You think you're so high and mighty. But I'll tell you something, Ash. You're not so clever as you think. Each man has a right to follow his own trail. Shambaugh might be a schemer. Don't think I'm blind to all his faults. But he has his uses. Like tonight, for instance.'

I squinted at him. 'What about tonight?'

'Shambaugh has ears in places we could never hope to listen,' he said. 'He hears things. Rumours. Plans. Plots.'

'What are you talking about?'

He stood up abruptly and reached for his shotgun. He said, 'Grab your rifle and come with me, if you want to live.'

'What?'

'And leave the lamp burning.'

Mystified, I took up my rifle and went with him out into the cool evening. Our long association was finally coming to an end. It could be measured in weeks now, maybe one single week, if things continued to go the way they were.

I drew in a deep breath to calm my temper. I felt disappointment and relief all in one. But evidently there were other matters to occupy us now. The torchlit street was as busy as ever, for Yellow Creek was a twenty four hour a day town. Up in the Badlands District I heard the occasional gunshot and scream, drunks laughing like hyenas and glass shattering like long friendships.

Jack indicated the row of stores directly opposite. 'Here,' he said.

We crossed the street and I followed him into a darkened alleymouth. 'What's this all about, Jack?' I asked.

'Just keep your mouth shut, take cover behind that rain-barrel and wait. You'll find out soon enough. And maybe then you might revise your opinion of Shambaugh.'

I did as he said. I could hardly remember a time when I had done anything else. The time was about seven-thirty. We hunkered there in the darkness, watching life go by, for about three-quarters of an hour. Then, suddenly, I stiffened, for I had heard the thunder of horses coming down the street at a hard gallop.

TEN

In the very next instant, four horsemen galloped into view with dirt flying up beneath their horses' driving hooves. They reached the cleared section just in front of our tent and hauled back on their reins, bringing their animals to a prancing, rearing halt. I looked from one man to the next, as they stood tall in their stirrups and drew their sidearms. They wore bandannas to hide their identities. But I knew from their attire and the easy way they handled their horses that they were not miners. Rather, they were gun-toughs, and Lord knew, there were plenty of those in Yellow Creek at the time.

They picked up high-paid work riding shotgun on the gold shipments sent out into civilisation.

I had guessed what they were going to do, but when they actually went and did it, I could not help but be stunned. They drew their sidearms and emptied them into our tent, doubtless believing that we were still inside it. I watched the bullets punch holes through the canvas, the tent itself shudder beneath the impact of the savage fusillade. *You sonsofbitches,* I thought. *You dirty, bush-whacking sonsofbitches.*

As I watched those four men who thought they were killing us, my grip on the Yellow Boy tightened and I began to bring the weapon up on them, determined to teach them a lesson they would not soon forget. But then Jack reached across and put a hand on the rifle's barrel, and when I looked around at him, he shook his head.

Suddenly the gunfire stopped. I returned my attention to those four horsemen of our own personal apocalypse. They wheeled their mounts around and blurred back up the street, yelling and shouting more out of some warped sense of excitement, I think, than anything else.

I knew why Jack had stopped me from opening fire on them. They had gone back the way they had come – towards the Badlands District. And there was no way out of Yellow Creek down there. Jack wanted us to follow them and find both them, and the man who hired the job done.

'Well,' he said, straightening up from his crouch and looking from me to our ragged, sorry-looking, shot-up tent. 'After that little display, I think even *you* will agree that Bob Shambaugh has his uses, Ash.'

I muttered something non-committal. 'Could you recognise any of them?' I asked.

He shook his head. 'No. But I'll remember their horses well enough the next time I see them. Two chestnuts, a black and a dapple grey.'

He set off up the street towards the District and I fell in beside him. For a moment it seemed like old times, Page and Colter, side by side against a common enemy. Townsfolk came running and started to congregate around the bullet-riddled tent. Glancing over my shoulder, I saw them pointing and speculating.

Up ahead, the Badlands District seemed to glow with the light of a million torches, and yet there was a brooding darkness up there that no amount of light could dispel. That area was a place of darkness, where the rotten part of every man could come un-ashamedly to the surface and enjoy every filthy, forbidden pleasure there was.

Life in the District was going on as normal when we finally got there. It was so noisy that they probably hadn't heard all the gun-fire. Every rough-built saloon was packed to the rafters. The tinny, discordant strains of a dozen pianos mingled together to form one awful, tuneless backdrop. We came to a stop and Jack said, 'Take the other side of the street. You know what to look for.' I knew, all right. Two chestnut horses, a black and that distinctive dapple grey.

I crossed the street and we went deeper into that hell-hole, inspecting all the horses tied to the racks outside each boozy establishment. We got halfway down the street and then I heard a whistle. Glancing around, I saw Jack beckoning me. I went over there and saw the four horses we were looking for, tethered outside a saloon called the Gilded Lily.

It crossed my mind that these would-be assassins must be either very confident or very dumb. If I had been in their place, I would first of all have made sure of my kill before having the gall to stick around the very town in which I had performed the deed. And yet there they were, those horses, and the chances were good that the riders themselves were inside the Gilded Lily. But what were they doing in there – buying drinks, or drawing their blood-money? I inclined towards the latter, for the Gilded Lily was owned by Sid Jessup, the very fellow whom Jack had fined heavily for sundry misdemeanours, and whose other saloon he had razed to the ground.

I looked at Jack. He was obviously thinking along the same lines as me. There was no love lost between the two of them. Jessup's operation was rotten to the core. A few months before, he had sold some home-brewed whiskey that was so strong it had blinded two men permanently, and when a few of their friends had turned up on Jessup's doorstep to demand restitution, Jessup's bully-boy barmen had gone at them with wheelspokes, killing one and crippling two others. His girls were cheap and his games were rigged – in fact, there wasn't much to choose between him or Shambaugh, save that Shambaugh was not quite so blatant about it, preferring to disguise all his cheating ways beneath a veneer of semi-respectability.

Jack's regular patrols had severely restricted Jessup's dirty operation. It must have been costing him literally thousands of dollars in lost trade, so he had the best reason in the world for wanting us dead.

We listened to the sounds of merriment coming from within the saloon. Lamplight spilled out through the smeared windows to puddle at our feet. We walked over to the batwings and looked inside. The air was thick with smoke and laughter. Blowsy per-centers were encouraging shaggy customers to buy overpriced, so-called 'champagne'. Miners formed queues up at the bar. Watching them, I shook my head. Did they *never* learn? We scanned the saloon for the men we were after, but couldn't see them. Perhaps they were in Jessup's office, at the rear of the building.

'Stay here, Ash,' Jack said quietly. 'I'll go around the back and see if I can't smoke them out.'

He strode away and down the trash-strewn dog-trot at the end of the building, leaving me to stand there in tense expect-ation. Any moment now I expected to hear a sudden explosion of gunfire but nothing came. I pushed into the saloon and stood just inside the batwings, keeping my eyes on the curtained doorway in the rear wall, beyond which lay Jessup's office.

Nothing happened. Then, suddenly, Jack pushed out through the curtain and I could tell by his expression that he had found the office empty.

He raised his shotgun and discharged both barrels right into the tin ceiling. Suddenly the saloon fell absolutely quiet as patrons and staff alike turned hurriedly to face him.

Jack broke open the shotgun, removed the two still-warm cases and tossed them to the floor. Smoke drifted lazily from the barrels to join the haze up around the lanterns. He took two fresh shells from his jacket pocket and reloaded, then snapped the weapon shut again.

'All right, gents,' he said quietly. 'Move along, if you will. This place is closing down. Permanently.'

There was some muttering. One of the barmen, a big-muscled, broken-nosed troublemaker from California, said, 'You got no reason to close us down, marshal.'

'Would you care to bet on that, Baker?' Jack replied. 'Now, come on, you men. There's plenty of other saloons to spend your money in. Move along, now.'

The miners cast surly looks his way. They didn't particularly care to have their fun broken up for them, but they knew better than to argue with a man toting a shotgun. Slowly, with questioning glances at each other to see who was going out first, they began to rise and file towards the swing doors. We watched them spill out into the night, still hoping to spot the men we had come in here for, but without success.

Sid Jessup came hurrying down from upstairs, straightening his attire. From his flushed look, it was obvious that he had been sampling the dubious delights of one of his girls. He was short and fat and forty years old. He had some Italian blood in him, and he was olive-skinned and very dark of eye, with a shining bald head surrounded by thick black hair, and a very thick beard. I never saw him in anything but a tailored grey suit and a purple silk vest, and that night was no different. He planted himself right there before Jack and said, 'What the hell do you think you're playin' at, Page?'

Jack said, 'I think you know damned well, Sid.'

'You got no right to close me down! What'd I ever do to you that you want to close me down, eh?'

Jack brought up the shotgun and hit him in the face with the butt, and I winced as Jessup screamed and fell backwards, both hands going up to his ruined nose.

'*You sonofabitch!*' he yelped. 'I'll kill you for that!'

And Baker, his chief barman, was already reaching under the bar for a wheelspoke in order to do just that, but as he came running, Jack turned the shotgun and fired one barrel, and Baker flew backwards into shelves filled with bottles of watered liquor, and went down in a shower of jagged glass and foul-smelling liquid, leaving part of his stomach and spine to congeal where he had connected with the wall.

Jack went upstairs. It was so quiet that I could hear the floorboards creaking as he checked each crib. A few moments later he came back down and said, 'Where are they, Sid?'

Holding his face, Jessup spat, 'I don't know what you're talkin' about, you bastard!'

'I'm talking about the four men you hired to kill us. I know they were here. Their horses are still tied outside.'

'Go to hell!' Jessup hissed. 'I don't know what you're talking about, Page. But if someone hired these fellers to kill you, I'm only sorry they didn't succeed!'

Jack went over and hit him again, and he went down with blood dribbling from his mashed lip to stain his chin with a crimson goatee. He swore as best he could, mopping his face with one sleeve, but shut up when Jack came to stand over him, and point the shotgun right at him.

'Whatever you paid them, it wasn't

enough,' Jack said softly. 'Because it doesn't mater how long it takes, Sid – I'll find them and settle with them all. You tell them that from me. Tell them that, and then get the hell out of town.'

Indignant colour came to Jessup's fleshy cheeks. 'What ... what...?' he blustered.

'You're through here,' Jack said through clenched teeth. 'I want you packed up and out of town by noon tomorrow. If you're still here and I see you, I won't ask why. I'll just shoot you on sight like the dog that you are!'

He came back to me and we pushed out through the batwings and then out through the crowd. It all caught up with me then, the tension I had been holding back. I just wanted to fall into my blankets and go to sleep, but we had nowhere *to* sleep, thanks to those bushwhackers, who were still on the loose.

We paused in the centre of the street. 'I don't know about you,' Jack said, breaking in on my thoughts, 'but I need a drink.'

I looked at him. He appeared tired, old,

somehow ill-used. 'At Shambaugh's place?'
I asked.

He nodded. 'At Shambaugh's place.'

We changed direction and went up onto the opposite boardwalk and right into the Prospector's Rest, and no sooner had we stepped inside than the four-piece band Shambaugh employed struck up 'For He's a Jolly Good Fellow' and the assembled patrons began to applaud.

I wondered what we – or, more likely, *Jack* – had done to deserve such a reception, but then I had it. We had closed Sid Jessup down, and news travelled mighty fast in the Badlands District.

Bob Shambaugh weaved effortlessly around the tables crowded into the big room, grabbed Jack by the hand and pumped it enthusiastically. Shambaugh was Jessup's complete opposite. He was tall and well-built, almost too handsome for his own good, with a thick head of dark hair, two deep, glittering brown eyes, a fine, straight nose and, for that time, perfect teeth. Like

Jessup, he always wore well-tailored suits, but unlike Jessup, he also wore a sidearm, a big, long-barrelled Peacemaker in a tooled brown leather holster.

'That was a fine thing you just did for Yellow Creek, Marshal Page!' he said. 'It's scum like Jessup give honest traders a bad name!' Then he turned to the crowd and said, 'Three cheers for the marshal!'

As someone yelled, 'Hip-hip,' and everyone else joined in with *'Hurrah!'*, I turned my attention to Jack. All the tiredness had disappeared from his face and his eyes had taken on a new shine. He was never happier than when he had an audience, and now it seemed to give him new strength to soak up all their adulation. Again I shook my head in wonder, for could he not see that all of this was false, that they were deliberately giving him what he wanted to have, just in order to buy his favour?

But then I remembered something that happened a couple of years earlier. It was the winter of '73, I believe, quite a harsh one in that part of Colorado, and it was so bad outside that we spent day after day in the marshal's office, just playing cards and swapping gab.

On this particular day, the conversation turned to the men we most admired, and there was a mixed bunch of them; Bear River Tom Smith, John Chisum, Sam Judge and the like. Our colleagues rapidly warmed to this topic, for we all knew or had met most of the men about whom we spoke, and each of us had a story or opinion to pass on them. But throughout that entire conversation, Jack remained silent, just toyed with a deck of cards, shuffling them, fanning them, flipping them into a pile and then gathering them up to do it all over again.

It was a subject that evidently held no interest for him, and when at last he did open his mouth to speak, it was only to say, 'For God's sake, you fellows – are we going to play cards or what?'

Only now did I understand why he had not joined in that day. It was because he had been waiting for one of us to place *him* alongside those other famous men. He knew we all considered him to be a living legend, but for Jack that wasn't enough. He did not want to be *one* of the best, but *the* best. And here, in the smoky, boozy atmosphere of Shambaugh's saloon, he was exactly that, the king, and these whores and cardsharps and stupid, drunken miners were his loyal subjects. Jack Page had come home, at last.

We stayed the night at the Prospector's Rest, in the surprisingly palatial suite Shambaugh had promised Jack earlier that day, and though it was not difficult to grow accustomed to such opulence, I made up my mind to find alternative accommodation the very next morning.

As tired as I was, however, I had trouble sleeping that night. There was something about Shambaugh's pretend *bonhomie* that made me feel uneasy. He was an out-and-out crook. He wanted to be the undisputed king of Yellow Creek. And, since we had closed down the operation of his biggest rival – Jessup – he was already one step closer to realising that ambition.

I lay awake, wondering about the four men who had shot up our tent that night. Who had *really* put them up to it? Jessup? He genuinely had not seemed to know anything about it. And surely he would not have been so careless as to allow his assassins to tie their horses right outside his saloon, clearly linking him with them.

Shambaugh, then? The very man who had 'warned' us of the attempt on our life? It was possible.

I knew I could not confide this suspicion to Jack. He and Shambaugh were already as thick as thieves. But I made up my mind to watch Shambaugh from here on in.

I rose early the following morning, washed, dressed and prepared to leave. As I strapped on my gunbelt, Jack watched me from the other side of the room, arms folded across his chest. 'Not even going to stop for a bite to eat, Ash?' he asked.

'I don't think so.'

'Too bad. Shambaugh employs a fine Chinese cook.'

I tied the thong around my leg and tested the hang of my gun. 'So,' he said. 'You're really serious about it, then? Going?'

I nodded.

'It must be comforting to possess such high principles.'

My response came out before I could stifle it. 'You should try it some time.'

He only shrugged. 'You're letting the child in you show, Ash,' he admonished.

I ignored the taunt and crossed to the door. 'So long, Jack. I daresay I'll see you around.'

I opened the door and went out into the hallway. He came out after me. 'I'll walk you downstairs,' he said.

The saloon was dark and empty, for it was still early. It stank of sweet, spilled alcohol and stale tobacco smoke and sawdust and vomit. We clattered downstairs and weaved between all the vacant, littered tables to reach the doors. Jack would be at home in this seedy atmosphere, I thought sadly, with whiskey and fat cigars never far away and, of course, his loyal subjects ever-ready to pander to his ego.

We stopped at the doors and turned to face each other. I saw him as if for the first time. He had let himself go. He did not look at all dapper in his creased white shirt and loud check pants, with his Remingtons stuffed into his crimson sash. He only looked like a faded memory of yesterday.

To my surprise, he stuck out his hand. 'Well,' he said, 'it's been a long road, Ash, but it looks as if we've finally reached trail's end. No hard feelings?'

I looked at him, at this man I had respected more than any man before or since, this man who had, over a period of time, become a complete stranger to me. I did not know if I wanted to shake with him, and never got the opportunity to find out if I would, for at exactly that moment, someone outside yelled his name, and I saw the slightest narrowing of his eyes and tightening of his lips as he turned away from me and unbolted the door, swung it open and walked out into the grey silence of early morning.

Sid Jessup was standing in the centre of the street, some thirty feet away. He was, as ever, encased in a tailored grey suit and a purple silk vest. His nose looked swollen and red and there was a big, ugly, blue-brown bruise on his cheek. Jack came to a halt at the edge of the boardwalk and stood with his legs slightly parted and his arms hanging loose and easy at his sides. I also went outside, and stood off a-ways, fearing yet more trouble.

Jessup had a tall, heavily-built fellow standing beside him. This was Red Hallenbeck, a gunfighter of some repute. Hallenbeck was a wolf-faced southerner in his mid-twenties, blond, with fierce, transparent blue eyes and a wicked, cruel smile forever on his lips. He stood a few feet off to Jessup's left, perfectly balanced, his left hand swinging gently above the butt of the worn-smooth .45 at his hip. He was widely known to be deadly slick with his gun, and not at all fussy about the uses to which he put it. On the surface, he was just another thug, but in another respect he was much, much more, because his skill with a gun and total lack of feeling made him a truly perfect killing machine.

'Good morning, Sid,' Jack said with a sociable nod. 'Come to pay your respects before leaving?'

Jessup shook his head. He looked like a dwarf next to Hallenbeck, who was at least six feet four, and there was an eager light in his eyes. 'Uh-huh,' he replied. ''Cause I'm not leavin', Page. You are. In a pine box.'

I sensed rather than saw the lift of Jack's eyebrow. 'Really?'

This time it was Hallenbeck who spoke. 'Yeah,' he said. 'Really.'

'Still hiring no-goods to try and kill me, Sid?'

'This is the first, Page,' Jessup replied. 'An'

the only one I'm likely to need.'

Jack shook his head. 'I didn't know you were in so much of a hurry to die,' he said.

'It's true I'm in a hurry,' Jessup sneered. 'But not to die, *marshal*. To shovel earth onto your ugly face.'

Jack considered that, then shrugged. 'Well,' he said. 'If you're set on it, let's get to it. Are you ready, Hallenbeck?'

I looked at Hallenbeck's death's-head grin and wanted to shudder. 'Ready an' waitin',' he replied, and went for his gun.

Two gunshots blended into one. Hallenbeck was faster by perhaps a second, no more. But being fast isn't enough. You have to be accurate, too – and Jack was both.

Hallenbeck's slug whistled past Jack's head and thudded into the log wall behind him. Jack's .44 caught Hallenbeck just above the left breast and knocked him backwards. He staggered like a drunk, wearing that same surprised look I had seen on all the other men Jack or I had killed. Then he brought his .45 back up for another shot but

Jack shot him again, and this time Hallenbeck twisted around and collapsed in the rough, muddy street.

I yelled Jack's name then, for I had seen Jessup reaching into his jacket, and Jack went down into a crouch and spun towards him. He fired both guns again and Jessup's eyes screwed tight shut and he yelled a curse, then fell over, a tiny hideout gun in his right palm.

We heard footsteps then, off to our left. Someone was racing towards us. As one we both turned to face this newcomer, but Jack did not wait to identify him, he simply fired two more bullets and the man who was coming at us was picked up and tossed aside, and it was only as he writhed in the dirt that Jack saw that he was in fact nothing to do with Jessup, just a middle-aged fellow by the name of Milligan who swept up in the next saloon along, an innocent bystander who had made a mistake of seeing what had happened and coming to offer assistance.

'Aw, Christ,' Milligan said through clenched teeth, hugging himself and rolling from his side onto his back. 'I'm kilt. God help me. I'm kilt...'

Jack stared down at him. He could have been a statue, for all the animation he showed. I shoved past him and went down into the street and forced Milligan to lay still. 'Easy now,' I said. 'Easy, now...'

It did not look good. He had taken both bullets in the centre of the chest. Blood was already flecking his taut lips. I looked over my shoulder. Jack was staring down at the man he had shot. His face was twisted and bloodless. 'Put that gun away,' I said in a low, hoarse voice. 'Get down here and give me a hand with him.'

He did as I said and we carried Milligan as gently as we could back into the gloomy saloon, ignoring all the people who had come to see what had happened. Shambaugh appeared on the staircase, a cigarette in his mouth. We stretched Milligan out on a table and I said, 'Fetch a doctor. Quick!'

Milligan was moaning again. I told him to lay still and breathe as deeply as he could. His heaving chest was a mess. Someone hurried past us and out into the street. I didn't see who it was, but I knew that Shambaugh had dispatched one of his minions to fetch the doctor. Jack was standing beside me. I heard his whispering, 'My God ... my God ... what have I done?'

'Easy now, Milligan,' I said. He was a grey-headed angular man with a lined face and big ears. Harmless, I thought. Wouldn't hurt a fly.

I began to unbutton his shirt. My hands were shaking and it was difficult. I loosened perhaps four buttons and then I realised that Milligan had stopped breathing. I froze. The realisation that he had just died struck me like a slap in the face.

I said his name, but there was no reaction. Milligan's eyes stared straight up at the ceiling. They still held a look of horror.

'What *have* I done?' Jack whispered. 'God, when this gets out...'

I turned to face him with a frown lowering my brows and a look of disgust souring the line of my mouth. I could hardly believe what I had heard. '*What?*' I asked. Then louder: 'What was that?'

He tore his gaze away from the body on the table and looked at me. 'I...' He struggled to find the right words. 'What are they going to say when they hear about this?' he asked, shocked and pale.

I had trouble taking it all in. I said, 'Do you mean to tell me that you've killed an innocent man and all you can find to worry about is your *reputation?*'

Everything came roaring to the surface then; my disappointment and frustration and disgust and the combined weight of every death I had caused and witnessed. I had not wanted to spend my life trailing about the country, living in someone else's shadow, I had wanted to live a good, honest life, but instead I had ended up rubbing shoulders with every degenerate low-life society could hope to throw up and I had

had enough of it.

I lashed out and punched him right on the jaw. His head snapped sideways and he staggered backwards to crash against one of the tables. He went down on his backside and stayed there, looking up at me, seeing an Ash Colter he had not dreamed could exist.

'Damn you!' he hissed, breathless. 'No man strikes me and gets away with it!'

I jabbed a finger at him and he actually flinched. 'And no man kills an innocent bystander in a town where I wear a badge,' I snapped back.

He looked sidelong at me, wary and cautious. 'What's that supposed to mean?'

I took a deep breath. 'It means that I've had enough of you, Jack. I've had you and your gun-happy ways up to here, and so have most of the good people in this town. So I'm posting you *out* of town, Jack, and if you've got any sense, you'll go and not come back, because by God, if you stick around, I'll see to it that you stand trial for murder!'

He got to his feet, blood showing at the corner of his mouth. 'Get down off your high horse, Ash!' he said impatiently.

'I mean it, damn you!' I answered. And I did. I reached out, took hold of the shield pinned to his shirt and tore it off, tearing the material along with it. 'You're not fit to call yourself the city marshal, Jack. So get out of town. Go someplace where your precious reputation's still intact, because as sure as hell it'll be worthless around here after this!'

For a long moment we glared at each other. I thought he might go for his guns again, or attempt to strike me, but he did neither. Instead he reached up, wiped the blood of his mouth with his shirtsleeve and said, 'You can't do this, Ash. You don't have the authority.'

'Then I'll *get* the authority.'

'Where?'

'From the people.'

He frowned. 'You mean hold an election? You're crazy!'

'I want you out of this town, Jack. And I'll

do whatever it takes to *get* you out. If you'd prefer to settle it right here and now, go ahead. You won't find me backing down.'

He looked at me strangely. He appeared genuinely confused and hurt. 'What's the matter with you, Ash?' he asked. 'We used to be friends.'

I shook my head. 'You used to be someone I could be friends *with*,' I replied bitterly, turning on my heel and heading for the batwings until his voice stopped me and I turned back to eye him expectantly.

He said, 'You talk a good fight, Ash, and I respect you for it. But I know you'd never go up against me. You know just how fast I am.'

I shook my head again. 'Don't put it to the test, Jack. It could just be the last mistake you ever make.'

ELEVEN

I went directly to Walter Murphy's rooms at the Sultan's Palace. As the unofficial mayor of Yellow Creek, I felt he should know what had happened. But as soon as he answered his door to my knock, a look of profound relief washed over his pale, jowly face and he said, 'Ah, Colter! The very man! I thought you'd never get here!'

He was clearly distraught as he led me to a horsehair sofa and bade me sit down. 'You've heard about the robbery, I take it?' he said.

I felt a worm of apprehension stir in my stomach, and temporarily set my own problems aside. 'What robbery?'

'Barney Ross sent a gold shipment out last night, bound for Rapid City. About half a dozen miles out of town it was ambushed.'

I thought about that. Barney Ross ran probably the only reliable freight operation in Yellow Creek. Once a month, on average, he transported most all of the miners' gold from a depository at the bank down to the assay office in Rapid City, where it was turned into hard cash. For security reasons, he hardly ever adhered to a set routine and would sometimes decide to make a run at an hour's notice in order to avoid the very thing that had evidently happened the previous night. Up to now, it was a system that had worked well.

'Anyone hurt?' I asked.

'Two of the men Barney had riding shotgun on the shipment were killed.'

'How many of them were there, these robbers?'

'The driver estimates between eight and a dozen of them.'

Allowing for the inevitable exaggeration, that meant roughly about six. 'Descriptions?'

Murphy shook his head. 'Nothing that will help you much. They wore bandannas across their faces, and standard range gear.'

'How much did they get away with?'

'Barney says gold to the value of forty thousand dollars,' Murphy replied. 'The miners are not best pleased, as you can imagine. I fear they will turn ugly if something isn't done soon.'

I muttered a choice word and considered what he had told me. First of all I must have a word with Ross, see who else knew that he had been planning to send out a shipment, then talk with the survivors of the ambush and see if I could piece together any clues that might help me find the men I was after.

'I'll get right onto it,' I said with a nod.

He stopped me at the door. 'Oh, by the way,' he said. 'I heard about that attempt on your lives last night. I trust both you and the marshal escaped unscathed?'

I turned my hat in my hands. 'Actually, Mr Murphy, it was about me and the marshal that I wanted to see you.'

'Oh?'

I told him as much of it as I felt he needed

to know, trying to stress all the while that I was not telling tales out of school, or putting him in a position where he would have to choose between one of us or the other, but I could tell by his expression that he didn't really like what he was hearing. At the end of it he said, 'Well, obviously I'm sorry to hear that you two have had words, but... Look, Mr Colter ... Ash... You have to see this from all sides. You and Marshal Page have done a commendable job cleaning up Yellow Creek, but for all that, it's still a rough and ready town. It's just not ready for an election yet.'

I sighed, for that was true enough, I supposed. But what was the alternative? Jack and I could not continue to enforce the law as a team. And in any case, I had practically been doing the job single-handed as it was, ever since Jack had fallen in with Shambaugh. One of us would have to quit. Perhaps it should be me.

'Have a word with the marshal when you've both had the chance to cool down,'

Murphy advised paternally. 'Why, you two have been partners for so long, I doubt that one could exist without the other.'

I clapped my hat onto my head. That was a thought I found troubling. 'Well, I'll do what I can about this robbery,' I promised vaguely.

'It's going to be hard,' he opined. 'I suspect the villains will probably be out of the territory by now.'

I went back out into the street and walked up towards the remains of our ragged tent in order to gather my gear. The town was bustling, as usual. Murphy was probably right, I thought. The robbers more than likely *had* quit the territory by now. I reclaimed my few meagre possessions and took them back to the Palace and booked myself a small, clean first-floor front room. Then I went to a little cafe where the food was good and ate breakfast. After that, I embarked upon my investigation.

I did not feel too optimistic about tracing the robbers, but at least it was something to do, some way of occupying my mind without continuing to dwell upon the rapid deterioration of my relationship with Jack. Down at his freight office, I found Barney Ross besieged by angry miners, all bent on claiming compensation for their stolen gold. He was beside himself with worry, and shed little further light on the matter. He did beg me to help him, however, and it was a pitiful thing to see. He carried no form of insurance and feared that the miners might suspect that he had engineered the robbery himself, and string him up for his duplicity.

'*Did* you engineer the robbery yourself?' I asked casually.

He glared at me. 'That's not funny, Colter.'

He ran a small operation, and the next fellow I spoke to was his clerk, a youngish fellow with a ruddy complexion and thick brown sideburns, whose name was David Tapply. Tapply was a sturdy-looking man in a tweed vest and sleeve protectors. He had been with Ross for eight months. He agreed that he had known exactly when Ross was intending to send out the ill-fated shipment, but categorically denied the implication that he might have let that privileged information slip. He had an honest look and there was something sincere in the answers he gave me, but I wasn't completely sure about him. I had seen Tapply many times down in the District. Rumour had it that he had fallen hard for one of the whores down there and had set her up in a little shack so that he could have her all to himself.

I will not bore you with the intricacies of such an investigation, for this book is not intended to serve so much as a chronicle of those wild times as it is about Jack Page. Suffice it to say that I spent much of that day and the days that followed trying vainly to find clues and crack the case. I saw nothing of Jack, which suited me fine. I wondered if he had actually left town, as I had ordered, but I doubted it. Word of Sean Milligan's accidental slaying spread slowly, but it was dwarfed by the bigger news of the robbery, and did not cause as much of a backlash as I had expected.

In the next few days Ross suspended his operation and went into hiding, and I cannot truly say that I blamed him. The mood of the miners remained ugly, and it manifested itself in an increased incidence of violence down in the District. In the week following the robbery, there must have been more than twenty street-fights between men who had lost their gold in the robbery and others who said it served them right for being foolish enough to trust someone like Ross in the first place. Sometimes these disputes resulted in murder; there were three knifings in that same period, and two shootings.

I came under pressure to do something to calm the mood, but was unsure as to exactly what. Doubtless Jack would have quietened them down with the sheer force of his will alone, but I was not he. And in any case, I had taken his shield away from him. He was just another civilian now.

One night I was patrolling the District

when a familiar looking fellow brushed past me and headed on up the street, obviously in some kind of a hurry. I paused a moment, watching him from the back, until I recognised who he was. 'Evening, Tapply,' I called out.

Barney Ross's clerk turned around with a start. 'Eh? Oh … evenin', Mr Colter. Sorry, I didn't see you there for a minute.'

I glanced up at the velvet, star-spattered sky. 'Fine night, isn't it?'

'I guess,' he allowed without much enthusiasm.

'Been visiting your girl?'

His response was a tired, bitter smile. He had boasted to anyone who would listen about what a swell girl he had found himself. Now it looked as if he regretted every word he had ever spoken about her. He shrugged elaborately trying to make whatever he was about to say sound of little consequence and I realised that he had been drinking. 'Aw, no. No. Sylvie finished with me,' he said. 'I'm surprised you haven't heard. Must be all over town by now.'

'Argument?'

'No. Well, kind of. It...' Another shrug. 'She just wasn't the marryin' kind, I guess.'

I nodded my understanding, and he went on, thinking that he had found a sympathetic ear. 'She said she didn't want to be tied down to any one man,' he complained. 'Said she didn't want me providin' for her any more, that she was goin' back to work at the old place, so she could keep herself and be beholden to no one.'

'Too bad,' I said.

He smiled fleetingly, no doubt feeling embarrassed and emasculated by the thing his Sylvie had done to him, and went on his way. I also continued my patrol until, about ten minutes later, I spotted Jack, Bob Shambaugh and a couple of Shambaugh's gun-hung, rough-looking cronies ambling down the walk towards me, chattering loudly. I watched them come closer, walking from flickering amber torchlight into shadow, then back into torchlight.

When they were about twenty yards away, one of them noticed me. I heard my surname muttered in a low voice, and as one they came to a halt. I stood looking at them, hardly recognising Jack for the change that had overtaken him. His waist had thickened and his face appeared bloated and too red. He muttered something to Shambaugh and the others and they all laughed, and then he came ahead towards me on his own, left foot, right foot, left foot, right foot, in that same unstoppable stride, until he came to a halt about five feet away.

'Good evening, Ash,' he said with a nod. 'Out taking the night air?'

I shook my head. 'Just doing my job,' I replied. 'Making sure the scum stays off the street.'

He glanced around, his head cocked to one side. The District was doing its usual best to wake up anyone within a fifty-mile radius who might be trying to sleep. 'You're not doing too well, are you?' he remarked.

'I can't be,' I replied. 'I told you to leave

town and yet you're still here.'

'I thought all of that was ancient history by now.'

'Tell that to Milligan's widow.'

I saw by the slight narrowing of his eyes that I had struck something deep inside him, some part of him that was still decent and able to be shamed. 'Step aside, Ash,' he said shortly. 'We have places to be.'

I stood my ground. 'I told you I wanted you out of town, Jack, and I meant it.'

His mouth thinned down. 'Step aside, I said, and don't bother me with your foolishness.'

I stayed right where I was. 'A man I once knew told me that I ought never to back down from any man ever again. I'm following his advice right now. Get out of town, Jack, and out of this territory, or I'll arrest you right here and now.'

His moustache stirred a little and I knew that a sarcastic smile had fixed itself to his lips. 'You haven't got the sand for it,' he said softly.

I shrugged. 'There's one way to find out.'

I took a step back and set myself right there before him, legs parted and slightly bent at the knee, hands out to my sides, the fingers of my right hand clawed a few inches above the butt of my guns, the very gun he had bought for me.

His face was unreadable. He said, 'You're bluffing.'

Again I said. 'There's one way to find out.'

I saw his expression turn stony then, beneath the flickering torchlight. I knew that he had never walked away from a challenge in his life, and would not start now. He followed my example, backing off a step, assuming a pose of perfect balance, flexing his fingers hungrily.

I watched his eyes. I felt sure that I was going to die within the next few seconds. But he had slowed down, grown careless, whereas I, if anything, had sharpened and speeded up.

I caught the movement of his Adam's apple as he swallowed. I saw the tightening of the flushed skin over his full cheeks. I waited. The minute I sensed that he would make his play, I knew exactly what I must do, throw myself to one side, bring out the .442 and blast him to death.

'Kill him, Jack,' one of Jack's cronies said behind him. I recognised the voice as Shambaugh's.

Jack blinked, and I felt a rush of gratitude, for the command had broken his concentration. Another of them said, 'Go on, Jack.' But Jack blinked again, and I saw the muscles in his face slackening off. His whole posture relaxed then, and he forced a smile onto his lips. 'Go on about your business, Ash,' he said. 'You're not worth bothering with.'

And he brushed past me and hurried on his way, leaving me to turn and watch him go, and wonder whether he had deliberately decided against calling my bluff because he did not want to kill me, or did not want me to kill *him*.

I concluded my patrol and started back towards the Palace, wondering if I should leave

Jack to his own devices or keep pushing him until he had no choice but to fight me. Could I take him? I was no longer the know-nothing kid at the Snake River Station. I had learned a lot and I had learned it well. But would that be enough? And, if it came to it, did I really *want* to wound or kill this man who had once been such a trusted companion?

'Mr Colter?'

I came out of my reverie and glanced up. I had been so deep in thought that I hadn't realised the hotel was right before me. David Tapply was standing in the doorway a few feet ahead, swaying a little. Alcohol had made his ruddy face look ruddier still, and I saw he was sweating hard and looking furtive.

I nodded warily. 'Tapply,' I said. 'Are you all right?'

He swallowed. 'Sure, I…' He licked his lips, struggled briefly with some inner dilemma, then reached a decision. 'Can I have word?'

I nodded.

He glanced to left and right. There were a few riders in the street and the odd passerby, but it was late, and Yellow Creek was about as quiet as it was ever likely to get. 'Can we walk?' he asked.

Again I nodded. He was as jumpy as a jackrabbit. He had something on his mind, for sure, and I was afraid to speak in case I scared him off. But maybe he just wanted to talk about his girl, as jilted men do when in their cups.

'It's about the robbery,' he said.

A tingle washed down over my face. 'Oh?'

I felt his eyes burning into my profile. 'You remember ... remember when you asked me if I might've let word of the shipment slip ... you know, by accident?'

'Uh-huh.'

'Well, I lied. I *did* tell someone.'

'Sylvie?'

He nodded. 'Only in passin'. I mean, you know. Sometimes a man will say things. Don't think I did it deliberate, or that I was in league with them robbers. I had nothin' to do with it.'

'But you think Sylvie might have passed

the information on?' I asked.

He shrugged. 'I don't know. I don't suppose so. But…' Again his fevered gaze burned into me. 'She was seein' other men, you know. All the whiles she was seein' me.'

'And this is your way of trying to get even with her?'

He pulled up sharp. 'That's a hell of a thing to say! I love that girl!'

'Not so loud, dammit!'

All the fire went out of him and he sagged a bit. 'I don't know if she passed it on or not,' he said defeatedly. 'I'm only tellin' you because, I don't know, Mr Ross's in a hell of a state, and I'm out of a job till this thing is settled and he can open up the business again…'

I looked at him. He looked sad and pathetic. I didn't really know what to make of him, but again he seemed sincere enough, albeit in that maudlin, very serious way that drunks have, and he had provided me with the only clue I had thus far been able to unearth.

'All right, Tapply,' I said trying not to sound particularly interested. 'I'll make enquiries, see what turns up.'

'You'll keep my name out of it, though?' he asked eagerly.

'If I can,' I agreed. 'Meantime, go back to your lodgings and shut yourself away for a while. And lay off the drink.'

He nodded obediently and made to turn away, until I stopped him with a question. 'Your Sylvie,' I said. 'Where does she work?'

'The Prospector's Rest,' he replied.

Shambaugh's place!

I nodded soberly. 'Thanks,' I said, giving nothing away. 'I'll be in touch.'

He weaved unsteadily away from me, as I thought about what he had told me. I wondered if his girl *had* talked, and if so, to whom. For a moment I considered turning around and going down to the Prospector's Rest right now, but then I rejected the notion. It would be better to brace Tapply's whore in the morning, while the rest of the District slept late. Instead, then, I went to my room, stripped down and crawled into bed.

I found sleep elusive that night, and was up with the sun the following morning. I washed, dressed, buckled on my gunbelt and checked the loads. I did not anticipate trouble, but in Yellow Creek, you could never be completely sure. On impulse I grabbed my rifle and stepped out into the street with the weapon canted over one shoulder.

Tapply had rented a little shack down behind all the saloons and gaming houses, and I went there first. It was a mean-looking place built right up against one of those steep, wooded slopes. I knocked on the door but received no answer. It was still early so it was possible that Sylvie was sleeping late, but when I peered in through one grimy window, I saw that the place was empty. Perhaps the girl had moved back into the Prospector's Rest. Many of them found it more convenient to lodge where they worked.

I cut through an alleyway and out into the District. The sky was watery grey, streaked with lighter-coloured clouds. Here and there smoke drifted from brick chimneys as breakfasts were cooked and coffee was boiled. A couple of dogs fought over scraps down at the farthest end of the street.

I made for Shambaugh's saloon, came up onto the boardwalk and saw with some surprise that one of the doors was standing half-open. That was a stroke of luck, I thought, for I would sooner slip into the place, find the girl and ask her a few questions as discreetly as I could than risk alerting the robbers if she *had* talked about the shipment.

I entered the darkened main room and came to a halt. Bob Shambaugh was standing with his back to me at the foot of the staircase in the rear wall, watching as the same two big men he had been with the previous night carried a fourth man down from upstairs.

In the shuttered twilight, I thought they were just getting rid of the last of the previous night's drunks, but then I recognised the slack, bedraggled figure as Jack, and saw with a sudden flare of anger that he had been badly beaten; beaten, in fact, to within an inch of his life.

Glancing down, I saw his gear piled up a little way off to my left, his fine beech saddle, the Greener shotgun, his saddlebags and war bag, both hastily and clumsily packed. Shambaugh was saying impatiently, 'Come on, for Crissakes, we haven't got all day.'

A floorboard cracked under my weight and suddenly their faces came up and around in my direction. I was sure I saw alarm show in Shambaugh's glittering brown eyes, until he cloaked it with something flatter and altogether more cunning. He forced a smile onto his face. It was broad but insincere, and revealed his very good teeth. He came a step towards me and held out one hand in greeting. On the surface he looked as elegant as always, but there was something about him, the redness of his knuckles, a slightly mussed look to his clothes and hair, that told me that he had inflicted much of the damage Jack had sustained.

'Colter!' he said affably. 'Don't be shy, man, come on in! Can I get you a drink or is it too early for you?'

I indicated Jack with a tilt of the jaw and said, 'What's been going on here?'

He glanced over his shoulder. I glanced at Jack as well. His head was hanging on one side and you could barely see his eyes for all the bruises and swelling. Dried blood rimmed one nostril and oozed from his mashed lips. His long hair hung shaggy about his face.

'Well, I'll tell you,' Shambaugh said conversationally. 'I got to thinkin' about what happened betwixt you and Page last night, Colter, and bein' a civic-minded soul, I thought you were probably right – Page *has* outstayed his welcome around here.'

If looks could kill, I'd have stopped his clock right there and then. 'So you beat him up?' I asked. 'And, what, figured to dump him someplace out in the hills, maybe?' I shook my head. 'And I thought you were two were such good buddies.'

272

'Well,' said Shambaugh. 'You know how it is. Things change.'

'They change pretty damn' quick from what I can see of it.'

A low, moist sound filled the silence and it was a moment before I realised that Jack had regained consciousness and was trying to speak. Shambaugh turned around and said to his men, 'For Crissakes get that fat old has-been out of here before he gives the place a bad name.'

They started to do that but I said, 'No,' and they froze again. Jack raised his head and tried to focus on me with his bleary, bloodshot eyes. His lips worked for a moment or two, but no sound came out. Shambaugh said, 'Look, Colter, he's not worth botherin' with…'

But my instincts were telling me that suddenly he *was* worth bothering with, and worth it very much. 'Set him down in a chair,' I said. 'It sounds to me as if he wants to talk.'

Once again Shambaugh showed his perfect teeth in an easy smile. 'Okay, Colter,' he said placatingly. 'Okay.' But even before the last word had left his lips, his hand was blurring for the Peacemaker at his hip, and suddenly all hell was breaking loose there in the gloomy saloon.

Confused, but not entirely surprised, I threw myself sideways and down as Shambaugh's gun flamed and the room filled with the sound of the detonation. His bullet whined overhead and slapped into the wall behind me as I worked the lever of the Yellow Boy, came up on one knee and fired back.

Shambaugh threw himself backwards, up and over the mahogany bar. I saw the merest flash of grey as he vanished on the far side. Then more gunfire punctured the early morning silence as Shambaugh's two hired thugs pulled their own guns and started blasting away at me, leaving Jack to collapse in the sawdust as they ran for the cover of the tables and chairs on the other side of the saloon.

I pulled the nearest table over onto its side, hunkered behind it and worked the Yellow Boy and fired again. I caught one of the bully-boys in the arm, saw him twitch and yell and crash into a table and some chairs and send the lot scraping across the floorboards in a wild jumble. Another bullet sizzled above me and smashed one of the shuttered windows with a sharp tinkle. I fired back at Shambaugh and missed. His other hired man came around a table twenty feet away and triggered his Army .44 and suddenly I was knocked backwards and my right shoulder was on fire.

This is it, I thought. *After all these years, it's finally happened. I've run out of string.*

I heard Shambaugh's man let loose some kind of a whoop and I dropped the rifle and rolled a few feet away and drew my .442 awkwardly with my left hand. Gunfire erupted somewhere overhead and splinters leapt from table-tops and wooden beams. I fired once, wildly, just to make them keep their heads down, aching with pain, wanting to scream with it. Shambaugh, confident now, came up behind the bar and fired at me again. I shot back and he ducked his head back out of sight. I heard a sound behind me and rolled, saw the heavy I had winged with my rifle. There was blood on his left arm but he wasn't out of it yet. He had been trying to creep up on my blind side. When he saw that I had heard him he froze for two vital seconds before he thought to use the .31 in his fist. By then I had shot him again and he lurched forward and sideways, blood spilling from his throat.

A familiar voice called my name. *'Ash!'* It was Jack.

I rolled back over, knocking Jack's gear with my legs, and fired once more, just to make Shambaugh and his other man keep their distance. *God,* I thought. *I've been hit.* Blood was coursing warm and sticky down inside my shirtsleeve. I was starting to go into shock, feeling cold and shaky. I was in a bad spot and I knew it, but I was damned if I'd go down without a fight.

Again Jack croaked, '*Ash!*'

I chanced a look around the side of the table. I saw him on his belly thirty feet away, pale, beaten, but conscious. He was gesturing urgently with his right hand. Shambaugh called out, 'Give it up, Colter. We know you're hit. Throw down your gun and we'll get you a doctor.'

Yeah, I thought. *And pigs might fly.*

I heard a floorboard creak again. Shambaugh's other man was trying to creep up on me, just like his buddy had tried. Again I glanced at Jack. Our eyes locked. His right hand continued to flex and gesture.

Another creak.

Shambaugh's voice. 'Come on out, Colter!'

Sweat trickled down into my eyes and I blinked it away irritably. Shifting my gun into my right hand, I reached behind me until my fingers touched Jack's piled gear. Without daring to look around, I searched until I found what I was after; Jack's Greener. Slowly I withdrew it from his belongings. It

277

made a soft, metallic, whispery sound.

'You must be hurtin' awful bad, Colter,' Shambaugh said, and I was. 'Give it up. We got you out-numbered.'

I set the Greener down on the floor, so that it was directly in line with Jack. Jack's face grew animated when he saw it. He nodded as best he could and flexed his fingers some more.

I heard the sound of a big man setting his weight down on an ill-fitting board, and swallowed. I figured I had the sonofabitch pinpointed fairly well. Again I looked around the edge of the table at Jack. Again it felt like old times, Page and Colter, united against a common enemy. I put my free hand on the Greener, knowing I must put everything I had into this shove.

Shambaugh again. 'Colter?'

'I'm here, Bob,' I said, trying to keep all the hurting and desperation out of my voice. 'I'm here.'

I shoved the Greener and it slid along the floor towards Jack with a heavy, scraping sound. I heard Shambaugh say, 'What–?' and then I came up from behind the table, snap-aimed on the big, ugly-looking gun-tough who'd managed to light-foot to within a dozen feet of me and fired the .442.

My bullet hit him in the chest and he grunted and his hands went to the wound and I shot him again and he fell sideways and smashed into a table which splintered beneath him. In that same moment Shambaugh stayed where he was, revealed from the waist up behind the bar, and that was where he was standing when Jack snatched up the Greener, rolled onto his side and let go both barrels.

Thunder shook the big room and Bob Shambaugh's too-handsome face exploded in a crimson spray and he hit the shelves behind him, smashed bottles there and then collapsed out of sight.

Silence descended upon the saloon.

'Ash...?'

I pouched my gun, got onto my hands and knees, and using the table for support, got to my feet. 'I'm here, Jack.'

I went over to him, feeling faint. I knew that people would start venturing closer now that all the gunfire had stopped. When they did, I would tell them to fetch a doctor, quickly.

Jack had rolled onto his back and propped himself up against the bottom stair. He watched me come and kneel beside him through slightly-glazed, sad-looking eyes. He looked ghastly. Forgetting my own pain, I wanted to weep for him. 'Lie still,' I said. 'You'll be all right.'

He nodded feebly. 'I know,' he husked. 'But … Ash. I was … wrong. I owe you … an apology. Shambaugh…' He shook his head. 'Bastard was as crooked as they come.'

'What happened?'

'He … he figured he could … do what he liked to the … people and … and get away with it, as long as he had the law in his … pocket. Oh, he never said it like that … not in so many words, anyway… Until last night. Then he gave me my … orders. Said I should get my badge back ... because without it I was of no ... use to him. I should get my badge back and settle things with you. Once and for all.'

I could guess the rest. He had likely summoned up what little decency he still retained and told him to go to hell, and they had beaten him up and would have gotten rid of him – permanently – if I had not happened upon them when I did.

'Sham ... baugh was behind the gold robbery,' he said weakly. 'I found that out last night, as well. Well ... confirmed what I already ... guessed. One of his girls...'

I put a hand on his arm. 'All right, Jack. Rest, now. I can put the rest of it together for myself.'

He closed his eyes. 'I'm sorry, Ash,' he whispered. 'I was a fool, wasn't I? A blind, vain fool.'

I nodded. 'That you were,' I agreed. 'But it's over now, Jack. All over.'

TWELVE

A week later I went to see Jack in his newly acquired room at the Sultan's Palace and we sat together like two old men, spinning yarns and remembering the old days. His hurts had been tended and there wasn't much of him that wasn't taped up, but he was mending fast, and that was good. After some rough surgery the bullet had been taken out of my arm and it would, I was assured, heal pretty well in time.

It was a fine, blue-sky day but there was a nip to the air, for autumn was already with us and soon we would be putting another year behind us. We drank coffee laced with whiskey and laughed and chatted and it was as if all the old enmity between us had never existed. We had recovered the stolen gold, which had been buried beneath a storage shed out behind the Prospector's Rest, and Barney Ross was back in business, but David Tapply, fearing that his part in the affair might one day become public, had quit town one dark night and was never seen again.

At the end of my visit I rose to my feet and finally said the thing I had been leading up to all morning. 'I'll be pulling out tomorrow, Jack. I figure I've been around Yellow Creek long enough.'

He took the news with a neutral expression. 'Headed anywhere in particular?' he asked.

I shrugged. 'Not really. But I'll know when I've gone far enough.'

We looked at each other. What had he said to me once? That we had travelled a long road, but we had finally reached trail's end.

After a moment he extended his left hand so that we could shake. I reached out without hesitation. 'Good luck,' he said. 'As soon as I'm finished healing, I plan to ride on myself.'

I never saw him again. I rode out of Yellow

Creek next day and never looked back. In time I found myself some good land down in Texas and I got a loan from the nearest bank and started a horse ranch. I left it a little late, but eventually I married a good woman and had three fine sons, who run the place now that I am no longer as spry as I once was.

Every so often I heard stories about Jack Page, but the one that pleased me the most was the report of his wedding, some time in late '78. He married a girl by the name of Helen Thomason. It seemed that she had once worked as a waitress in a little eatery up in Le Quince, Nebraska, and had saved his life during the War.

When people learn of my association with Jack, they most often ask me why we did not continue to ride together once we had patched up our differences. By way of answer, I point to an event that happened just after I left Yellow Creek. I had gone perhaps four miles when suddenly I noticed a band of horsemen watching me from the edge of some timber away to the west. Seeing me, they broke cover and galloped down on the trail and fanned out ahead of me. There were about eight or ten of them, and their mode of dress – conch-shell breastplates, skin leggings etched with fine beadwork, and black bodypaint – clearly identified them as Sioux Indians.

My heart sank, for I had had my fill of killing, and knew that I could not hope to put up much resistance, not against those odds, and with my gun-arm still hanging in a sling. For a moment I considered turning my horse around and heeling it back the way I had come. I might stand a chance if only I could out-distance them.

I reined in about fifteen feet away from them and we sat our mounts looking at each other. I reached my left hand across my body to grasp the butt of my sidearm. My heart was pounding, for they looked a fearsome bunch. But I need not have worried, for after a time, one of them kneed his pony forward and raised one hand, palm out, and in pidgin English he said, 'Go in peace, white man. We know you. You are Colter. We have heard tales of your courage, and have no fight with you.'

That surprised me, because I had never considered myself to be any kind of celebrity. But I was not about to argue with them. Instead I nodded, and when they opened a path for me, I heeled my horse into a trot, and continued on my way.

That is why I did not continue my partnership with Jack Page. Because time had changed and things had changed and, most of all, *people* had changed. We were no longer man and boy, teacher and pupil, and Jack understood that now. We were, each of us, men of separate and distinct identity. Equals. And yet *more* than equals. Legends. Living legends. *Gunsmoke* legends.

The publishers hope that this book has given you enjoyable reading. Large Print Books are especially designed to be as easy to see and hold as possible. If you wish a complete list of our books please ask at your local library or write directly to:

Dales Large Print Books
Magna House, Long Preston,
Skipton, North Yorkshire.
BD23 4ND

This Large Print Book, for people
who cannot read normal print,
is published under the auspices of
THE ULVERSCROFT FOUNDATION